SCHOLA[STIC]

YEAR[IN] SPORTS 2025

ISBN 978-1-5461-3157-1

10 9 8 7 6 5 4 3 2 1   25 26 27 28 29

Printed in the U.S.A.   40
First edition, January 2025

Produced by Shoreline Publishing Group LLC

Due to the publication date, records, results, and statistics are current as of mid-August 2024.

Contents

Une Super Année!

That means "A Great Year!" in French! Why French? Because we are still calming down from two weeks of Summer Olympic Games in Paris that were *fantastique*! The golden moments and incredible athletes of the Olympics are the big highlight of this new edition of the YEAR IN SPORTS!

A memorable Opening Ceremony kicked off the Games in Paris, with athletes floating down the River Seine! For the next two weeks, viewers around the world thrilled to record-setting performances, dramatic finishes, and joyous celebrations. American fans had lots to cheer about, including the gymnastics GOAT, **Simone Biles**, the greatest female swimmer ever in **Katie Ledecky**, and the talent-packed US women's and men's basketball teams, both of whom won gold. Team USA once again led the world in Olympic medals, with at least one in 27 different sports!

When the Games finally ended (and did you see **Tom Cruise** dive into the Closing Ceremony before racing away on a motorcycle?!), everyone was left with memories for a lifetime. We hope we captured some of them starting on page 14.

But the Olympics was just part of a world-spanning year of action. Soccer fans were thrilled to watch European and South American championships that both ended with dramatic final games. Champs were crowned on other continents, too, as soccer continued as the world's most popular sport.

The gymnastics GOAT, Simone Biles, and her four new medals!

Was this the men's best basketball team ever?

Back here on home soil, fans saw several first-time champions. The Texas Rangers won their first World Series, while NY/NJ Gotham FC won its first NWSL championship. The Florida Panthers were first-time Stanley Cup winners. Speaking of hockey, the year also saw the debut of a new league, the Professional Women's Hockey League. Whichever team won the PWHL would be a first-time champ, too, of course—congrats to Minnesota!

Other champions were more familar. The Kansas City Chiefs became the first team since the 2003–04 New England Patriots to win back-to-back Super Bowls. Connecticut won its second straight men's college basketball title. In the women's tournament, South Carolina was also a two-fer, but skipped a year, winning in 2022 and 2024. The Boston Celtics won their 18th NBA title, setting a new all-time record for the league.

Plus we watched champions in lots of individual sports on courts, courses, and tracks.

All their stories, and many more, are just ahead. So strap on your reading sneakers, get to the starting line . . . and GO!

The Rangers danced for joy!

THE SPORTYS

Presenting the First-Ever
YEAR IN SPORTS
Awards!

All through this book, you'll read about most valuable players, and players of the year, and rookies of the year, and more. Those are the awards that get the most attention. Leagues and teams give them out to honor the best of the best in sports. Here at the *Year in Sports*, we've decided to expand on that a bit. This new section includes awards that we think *should* have been given. "The Sportys" honor athletes, teams, and events that stood out from the crowd in world sports from August 2023 to August 2024. Some made the news . . . others, well . . . not so much. Congrats to all the winners! Let us know if you think of others!

THE "WELL, IT'S ABOUT TIME!" AWARD
The WNBA Breaks Out . . . Big Time!

Caitlin Clark helped women's basketball have a big moment in 2023 . . . and it just kept growing! The WNBA has been around since 1997 but had its best and biggest year ever in 2024. Superstars like **A'ja Wilson** and 2024 rookie heroes Clark and **Angel Reese** helped, but so did a new TV deal that let more fans watch. Overall, women's sports is growing a lot. There is more attention in the media and more sponsorship money coming in. Who knows what's next?

Reese (left) and Clark lit up the league.

A MOST IMPORTANT MOMENT AWARD

Negro League Stats Added to MLB.

Baseball has been around for more than 150 years. For most of that time, nearly all the pro players were white. Black people did play in the late 1800s, but mostly on separate teams. In 1920, Black teams formed the first Negro League, a way to play pro baseball because Major League teams did not allow them to join. It was a racist stain on the nation's game, and it lasted until 1947, when **Jackie Robinson** broke the "color barrier."

From 1920 to the 1950s, the Negro Leagues included some truly remarkable players. And in 2024, something else remarkable (and overdue) happened. MLB finally added the history of Negro League players to the official MLB stats. Though the stories of heroes like **Josh Gibson**, **Oscar Charleston**, **Norman "Turkey" Stearnes**, and **Satchel Paige** are well-known to baseball historians, now even more fans will know their names. Check out these new lists of all-time leaders, and visit your library to find out more. They are the best . . . the new number ones!

A great catcher, Gibson is now No. 1!

CAREER BATTING AVERAGE

1. **Josh Gibson, .372**
2. Ty Cobb, .367*
3. **Oscar Charleston, .363**
4. Rogers Hornsby, .358
5. **Jud Wilson, .350**
6. **Turkey Stearnes, .348**

CAREER OPS**

1. **Josh Gibson, 1.177**
2. Babe Ruth, 1.164*
3. Ted Williams, 1.116
4. Lou Gehrig, 1.079
5. **Oscar Charleston, 1.062**
6. Barry Bonds, 1.051

Negro League players in bold type   * Former No. 1   **OPS: On-Base Plus Slugging Percentage

THE GOATIEST GOAT AWARD

Simone Biles Sets a New Standard.

She was already the best gymnast of all time, but in 2024, she vaulted even higher. After winning her ninth US championship, at the Summer Olympics in Paris, she won gold all-around, team, and vault, plus silver in floor exercise. Her career total of 11 Olympic medals, seven of them gold, is the most by a US gymnast.

THE "CAN HE DRIVE US TO SOCCER PRACTICE?" AWARD

Verstappen Laps the Formula 1 Field.

Formula 1 zoomed to new popularity in 2023. On the track, Dutch driver **Max Verstappen** zoomed to a new record. The series had 23 races . . . and he won 19 of them! It was probably the best season ever by a motor sports racer.

THE STICK-WITH-IT AWARD
Purdy Goes from Last to (Nearly) First.

This award is for every kid who gets picked last in gym class. San Francisco 49ers quarterback **Brock Purdy** was the final player chosen in the 2022 NFL Draft. But in the 2023 season, he led his team to the Super Bowl. They lost in overtime to the Kansas City Chiefs, but Purdy's amazing rise in his sport is a great example of sticking with it, no matter what!

ROOKIE LEAGUE OF THE YEAR AWARD
Welcome to the PWHL!

Sports leagues give awards to rookie players. We're giving one to a whole league! The Professional Women's Hockey League began skating in January 2024. Its six teams put on some action-packed games with thrilling overtime finishes. Minnesota was the first champ, but watch for even more from the PWHL in the future!

PWHL hockey is action-packed; watch for it in 2025!

BIGGEST UPSET IN A SPORT YOU PROBABLY DON'T HEAR MUCH ABOUT

USA! USA! USA!

While Americans were watching football or baseball or basketball, more than a billion people around the world were thrilled by cricket! Not the insect—the sport. But because so many people from around the world live in the US, the sport's T20 World Cup was held there in 2024. In one of the biggest upsets in the sport's history, the US team beat Pakistan in an early-round game! (Bonus: India ended up as the champion.)

SECRET SUPERSTAR AWARD

Yes . . . It's a Sport (Kinda).

A poll taken in 2023 revealed a surprise: America's most played sport is cornhole! Not swimming, not bowling; it's cornhole! It's a sport anyone can play, but one of the best is not much older than you. **Eian Cripps** is a nationally ranked pro and he's only 14!

US batsman Monank Patel goes for six (look it up)!

THE ROUND AND ROUND AND (ALMOST) ROUND AWARD

Trew Goes for 2.5!
Skateboarders need to know their geometry! Spinning in a circle means moving 360 degrees. Spin two and a half times and you've gone through 900 degrees. It's a tricky move to do on a skateboard. In 2024, Australia's 14-year-old **Arisa Trew** became the first woman to complete a 900!

THE BACK-TO-BACK-TO-BACK-TO-BACK AWARD

Oklahoma Goes for Four!

In 2024, the University of Oklahoma softball team dogpiled after setting a new college record when it won the national title for the fourth time in a row (count the "backs"). Pitcher **Kelly Maxwell** led the way with three wins and a key save. It was the Sooners' eighth title overall.

THE RAN OUT OF TIME AWARD

Nationals Run Out of Time.

In 2023, Major League Baseball added a pitch clock. Pitchers need to throw before a clock runs out. If they don't, the ump will award the batter a ball. But it was not until June 2024 that a game ended on a "clock-off." Washington's **Kyle Finnegan** ran out of time and ball four was called by the ump (right). That meant a bases-loaded walk scored the winning run for the Colorado Rockies.

THE RACCOON WHO THOUGHT IT WAS MESSI AWARD

A Four-Legged Soccer Player?

In a May 2024 Major League Soccer game, there was a timeout. That's rare in soccer, but the reason was even weirder. A raccoon had invaded the pitch! While the Philadelpha Union and NYCFC waited, stadium workers chased the raccoon for several minutes. Maybe it was just looking for a better seat?

BEST PLACE TO PLAY
Vive le Volley-ball!

The Paris Olympics had athletes playing in some amazing and beautiful places. But one of the sites was by far the coolest. (Okay, not really the actual coolest; temperatures rose to nearly 100 degrees Fahrenheit!) Let's say, the most beautiful. Beach volleyball was played on a temporary court built right below the Eiffel Tower!

CELEBRATION OF THE YEAR
Seriously . . . Watch the Video!

When you have spent years training for just one big moment . . . and when your dreams come true and you win an Olympic medal for your country—celebrate! And no one celebrated quite like Polish fencer **Aleksandra Jarecka**. When she clinched a bronze in team épée for her nation, she screamed, cried, jumped, fell, rolled, cried again, and more. Her joy spread and soon her whole team joined her, making one of the Olympics' most memorable moments.

A RIVER OF GOLD

The Opening Ceremonies for the Paris Olympic Games were one of a kind. As hundreds of thousands of fans cheered, all 206 teams floated down the River Seine in a fantastic watery parade that included cruising by the Eiffel Tower! The unique ceremony kicked off a two-week Summer Olympics that included thrills, drama, joy, and a thousand memories. We can't capture it all . . . but in this section, we sure gave it our Olympic best!

2024 SUMMER OLYMPICS

MAGNIFIQUE!

The beautiful Grand Palais, home to fencing, was just one of the amazing Paris sites.

What a fantastic Summer Olympic Games! They were truly *magnifique*! The Games in Paris began with the memorable Opening Ceremonies on July 26. The teams filled boats big and small and floated down the historic River Seine. Even a rainstorm could not put out the golden smiles and the Olympic flame. Dancers and singers and a mysterious masked torchbearer put on a show that crossed the whole city! The flame then rose in a hot-air balloon to burn above Paris until August 11!

The Games in Paris was also the first time that the number of men's and women's athletes was equal!

On the fields and in the stadiums, the athletes put on show after show. This section covers all the highlights, from Simone Biles' new gymnastics medals to Katie Ledecky's record-setting swim to the top of the all-time list. America still has the "world's fastest man" (Noah Lyles) and the best men's and women's basketball teams. The women's soccer team returned to the top as well.

Shot-putter Ryan Crouser set a new Olympic first, while cyclist Kristen Faulkner

FINAL MEDAL COUNT
(Top Five)

COUNTRY	G	S	B	TOTAL
1. USA	40	44	42	126
2. China	40	27	24	91
3. Great Britain	14	22	29	65
4. France	16	26	22	64
5. Australia	18	19	16	53

broke a 40-year US Olympic drought. Cole Hocker and Quincy Hall made amazing comebacks to win track gold. After the men's 4x100-meter relay team lost, the women's team sprinted to gold!

Of course, it was not just the US athletes. Swedish pole vaulter Mondo Duplantis thrilled a packed stadium by setting a new world record after he had clinched his second straight gold medal. Chinese swimmer Zhang Yufei led all athletes with six medals—but no golds! Arisa Trew won skateboarding gold for Australia—and she's only 14 years old! Several countries welcomed home their first-ever Olympic gold medalists (see box).

As the host country, France helped its athletes have a great Games. The nation discovered a new star in swimmer Leon Marchand and saw its teams win gold in men's rugby sevens and silver in

First-Timers

These athletes will always be the first Olympic gold medalists in their nation's history.

Saint Lucia: Julien Alfred, 100 meters

Dominica: Thea LaFond-Gadson, triple jump

Guatemala: Adriana Ruano, trap shooting

Dominican Republic: Marileidy Paulino,* 400 meters

*First gold medal by a woman

men's and women's basketball.

Most of the sports were held in Paris, but one was in far-off Tahiti, which is a long-distance part of France. The surfing event glided along a famous wave called Teahupo'o, with America's Caroline Marks and France's Kauli Vaast earning the gold medals for their skills on the boards.

When the torch finally went out on August 11, fans around the world said *au revoir* (goodbye) to Paris . . . but also *merci beaucoup* (thank you very much)!

Breaking! New Sport!

At every Olympics, local organizers can add sports. For Paris, it was breaking (once called breakdancing). Athletes show their physical skill and creativity, moving to fast-paced music. Ami Yuasa (right) was the women's winner, while Phil Wizard of Canada was the men's.

Yes, they are real! The US women's team made sure after they won the gold medal in Paris.

Gymnastics
US Back to the Top!

Simone Biles, Jade Carey, Jordan Chiles, Suni Lee, and Hezly Rivera made up the US women's team. All but Rivera took part in the team final. Each had to be at her very best against a tough field of competitors. But they all came through, and the US women won gold. It was a big comeback after a disappointing 2021 Olympics, where they won "only" silver. As she did in 2016, Biles led the way with amazing routines, showing that she was fully back from having to miss the 2021 team event. Italy was a surprise silver medalist, earning its first team medal since 1928! Brazil earned the bronze.

MEN'S GYMNASTICS

Superman clinched a bronze medal for the US team. Well, **Stephen Nedoroscik** (left) is not really a comic-book superhero, but he did earn the final points the team needed on the pommel horse. Why Superman? Like Clark Kent, Nedoroscik has to remove his glasses before flying to the rescue! He joined his teammates **Paul Juda**, **Brody Malone**, **Asher Hong**, and **Frederick Richard** on the podium. (Nedoroscik also got a bronze in the pommel horse event final.) Japan and China won team gold and silver.

SIMONE SOARS!

The greatest gymnast in history put on a show in Paris. **Simone Biles** had another dominant Olympic performance with three golds and one silver.

All-Around: Gold

In the all-around, the top 24 women take on all four gymnastics skills. The top total score wins. After the first two events, though, Biles was not in first place. A small mistake on bars had cost her points. After the balance beam, she was back on top. In the final event, floor exercise, three gymnasts had a shot at third place. American **Suni Lee** nailed her routine and earned a bronze to go with her gold from Tokyo. Going for gold, Brazil's **Rebeca Andrade** was excellent, and then it was up to Biles. She had to score at least 13.8 points to pass Andrade. As her family and a host of US celebrities watched from the stands, Biles soared, spun, and sparkled. She got 15.066 points . . . and the gold medal, adding another page to the greatest career in gymnastics history.

Vault: Gold

Biles performs a vault that no other woman has ever even tried. In the vault

Biles once again thrilled her many fans!

final, she ran, leaped, spun, and landed with another gold medal.

Floor Exercise: Silver

In the final individual event, Biles made two small errors, stepping out of bounds after landing at the end of tumbling runs. Andrade capped off her own great Olympics with a gold; Biles earned silver.

Other American Medals

Congrats to **Suni Lee** (left) for winning a bronze medal in the uneven parallel bars. Her teammate **Jade Carey** got a bronze in the vault, too.

Swimming & Diving

Queen Katie . . .

American swimmers led the way with 28 total medals, including eight gold. One of the biggest stories was the ongoing amazing story of **Katie Ledecky**. She won the 1500-meter freestyle race (she also won in 2021), setting a new Olympic record. That win joined an earlier bronze in the 400 free. Then she added silver in the 4x200-meter freestyle relay. And she capped off another incredible Games with a gold in the 800-meter freestyle—her fourth win in that event! That gave her a career total of 14 Olympic medals, the most ever by an American woman athlete. Also, her nine gold medals are tied for most all-time by a woman in any Olympic sport. Guess what? She said she's planning on returning to the Olympics in Los Angeles in 2028 . . . so keep your eyes on the pool!

. . . and Her Court!

Other US gold-medal winners included:
- **Kate Douglass**, 200-meter breaststroke
- **Bobby Finke**, 1500-meter freestyle (world record!)
- Men's 4x100-meter freestyle relay
- Women's 4x100-meter medley relay
- Mixed 4x100-meter medley relay (world record!)

Huske's golden look of surprise!

Persistence!

In 2021 at the Tokyo Olympics, **Torri Huske** missed a medal by 1/100th of a second. That's faster than an eyeblink! In Paris, she proved that sticking with it pays off, winning five medals to tie teammate **Regan Smith** for most on

Katie Ledecky

Marchand thrilled Parisian fans!

Kaylee McKeown upset favored US swimmer Regan Smith to win the 100-meter backstroke. The Aussies also won the women's 4x100-meter and 4x200-meter freestyle relays.

International Notes

German Star: Lukas Märtens won gold in the 400-meter freestyle. It was the first medal ever in the event for Germany.

Double Gold for Italy: Two Italian swimmers won races—Thomas Ceccon in the 100-meter backstroke and Nicolò Martinenghi in the 100-meter breaststroke.

Record Breaker: China had a great Games. Pan Zhanle set a world record in winning the 100-meter freestyle. In the 4x100-meter medley relay, his anchor leg was just fast enough to win gold over the US team. It was the first time the US had ever lost that Olympic race!

Swedish Splash: Sarah Sjöström won the 50- and 100-meter freestyle races.

the US team! She surprised favored teammate Gretchen Walsh, the world record holder, to win gold in the 100-meter butterfly. Walsh got the silver. Huske won golds in the mixed and women's 4x100-meter medley relays. She won silver in the 100-meter freestyle and the 4x100-meter freestyle relay.

Hometown Hero

Perhaps the biggest swimming star of the Paris Games was France's own Leon Marchand. He won the 400-meter individual medley early in the first week, setting off a big celebration. Then, in a single afternoon, he won the 200-meter butterfly *and* 200-meter breaststroke gold medals. He capped off an amazing Games with an Olympic record while winning the 200-meter individual medley.

Aussies! Aussies!

The Australian team had one of its most successful Olympic Games ever, with 18 medals including 7 gold. Ariarne Titmus beat rival Ledecky to win gold in the 400-meter freestyle. She also got silver in the 4x200-meter freestyle relay and silvers in the 200-meter and 800-meter freestyle.

Titmus even beat Ledecky in one race!

Track & Field

SPRINT CHAMPS: American **Noah Lyles** won the 100 meters by only .0005 seconds. Officials needed a photo to see who won. **Gabby Thomas** won the women's 200 meters, adding to the bronze she won in 2021. In the women's 100 meters, American **Sha'Carri Richardson** just missed out on a gold, losing to **Julien Alfred** of Saint Lucia by only 0.15 seconds. But Richardson led the 4x100-meter relay team to a big win!

UPSET!: American runner **Cole Hocker** picked the right time to run the best race of his life. He won the 1500 meters in a huge upset over defending champ **Jakob Ingebrigtsen** of Norway. Hocker was in fifth place with 300 meters to go but put on a huge sprint to win. Teammate **Yared Nuguse** won the bronze.

It was the first time since 1912 that two Americans earned medals in this famous race.

HEAVY HISTORY: American world record holder **Ryan Crouser** became the first man ever to win three straight golds in shot put. More history was made in the hammer throw when **Annette Nneka Echikunwoke**'s silver was the first medal by an American woman in that spinny sport. **Valarie Allman** won her second discus gold in a row.

LEAPS AND VAULTS: Americans leaped to medals. **Tara Davis-Woodhall** soared to the long jump gold. (She stayed in France to watch her husband, **Hunter Woodhall**, compete in the Paralympics!) **Katie Moon** earned a silver in the pole vault to go with the gold she won in Tokyo in 2021.

HURDLE HEAVEN: Sydney **McLaughlin-Levrone** had already set the world record in the 400-meter hurdles five times.

Ryan Crouser

Sydney McLaughlin-Levrone

5000- and 10,000-meter races, a rare double play! Hassan won bronze in those two long races, and then she won the marathon! Her Paris total distance was more than 35 miles!

* Morocco's **Soufiane El Bakkali** defended his 3000-meter steeplechase gold. America's **Kenneth Rooks** was a surprise bronze medalist. This tough event includes a long run, but also four hurdles each lap, plus a hurdle over a pool of water!

So it was no surprise that she did it again in Paris. Her time of 50.37 seconds put her well in front of the silver medalist, US teammate **Anna Cockrell**.

WORLD HEROES:

* Belgium's **Nafi Thiam** became the first woman ever to win the heptathlon (seven events over two days) gold medal three times! Decathlon champ **Markus Rooth** of Norway finished all 10 events of the difficult decathlon to earn that gold medal.

* Great Britain's **Keely Hodgkinson** kicked away from the field to win the challenging 800-meter run.

* **Beatrice Chebet** from Kenya and **Sifan Hassan** of the Netherlands ran a *looonnng* way! Chebet captured gold in both the

Soufiane El Bakkali

Basketball

Diana Taurasi set a record with her sixth Olympic gold medal.

WOMEN'S

If there was one medal the US was destined to win, it was this one. American women had won 56 straight Olympic basketball games heading into Paris. The streak reached 61 when they defeated France to win the gold again! No team has ever won that many in a row! Along the way, they beat Japan, Belgium, Germany, Nigeria, and Australia. The final was close, however. France played the US tough. The last shot of the game pulled France to within one point. It missed being a three-pointer when the shooter put her foot on the shot line. The US won 67-66.

MEN'S

On their way to gold, the US won all its pool play games, then swamped Brazil by 35 points in the quarterfinals. In that game, **Kevin Durant** had 11 points and became the America's career Olympic scoring leader. In the semifinal against Serbia, **Stephen Curry** poured in 36 points and **LeBron James** had a triple-double. The US needed them all—the Americans trailed by 17 points but came back to win 95-91. In the gold-medal game against France, Curry nailed four three-pointers in the fourth quarter to clinch a 98-87 win.

8

That's how many Olympic championships the US women have won in a row. They have 10 all-time . . . out of the 13 golds ever awarded!

Curry was clutch in the gold-medal game.

Soccer

WOMEN'S

Back on top! After missing out on gold in the past two Olympics, the US women won gold in Paris. The team swept through pool play. They beat Zambia 3-0, with **Mallory Swanson** scoring twice. The Americans swamped Germany 4-1 in a real statement game. **Sophia Smith** had a pair of goals in that one. A hard-fought 2-0 win over Australia made the US tops in their group. In the quarterfinal, **Trinity Rodman** smacked in a great extra-time goal to beat Japan 1-0. Smith did the same against Germany in the semis, scoring the only goal to earn a spot in the gold-medal game. Facing Brazil, the US had a tough fight. But a goal by Swanson in the second half put them ahead. The defense held, led by goalie **Alyssa Naeher**, and the US earned its first gold in soccer since 2012 with a 1-0 win.

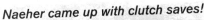

Naeher came up with clutch saves!

Swanson got a lift from Lindsey Horan.

BOX

MEN'S For the first time since 2000, the US men advanced into the Olympic quarterfinals. The under-23 team played surprisingly well. Though they lost to France in the opener, they looked strong in a 4-1 win over New Zealand—that was the most goals by a US team in an Olympic match! A 4-0 loss to Morocco in the round of 16 ended the Games for the US. Spain won the gold, beating France in the final.

American Heroes

What an Ending!: In one of the Paris Games' most stunning moments, the US women shocked Australia to win bronze in rugby sevens. On the last play of the game, **Alex "Spiff" Sedrick** sprinted 90 yards for a tying try. A two-point kick after the try made the Americans 14-12 winners over the No. 2 team in the world! The game helped cap off an entertaining, stadium-packed tournament for this exciting event.

Golden Foils: Americans are really improving in the ancient sport of fencing.• **Lee Kiefer** won her second straight gold in the foil event. Teammate **Lauren Scruggs** earned the silver after losing to Kiefer in the final. Then, led by Kiefer, the US won its first gold medal ever in the women's team foil!

On Target: Other than the "big three" (gymnastics, swimming, and track), the US won its most medals in shooting, with five. Leading the pack was **Vincent Hancock**, who picked up gold in skeet and a silver with **Austen Smith** in team skeet.

The Final Arrow: **Brady Ellison** made it to a shoot-off with South Korea's

Sedrick raced to an upset win!

Eaton soared high for silver in skateboard street.

Kim Woojin in the archery final. Ellison shot a 9, but Woojin's arrow was a 10. Ellison won the silver, his fifth career Olympic medal.

Dude! Medals!: Jagger Eaton

and Nyjah Huston earned silver and bronze in skateboard street. It was a big medal for Huston, one of the oldest and most successful skaters, who had missed a medal at the Tokyo Games after a fall.

Rowing to Gold:
Nick Mead, Justin Best, Michael Grady, and Liam Corrigan finished fifth in the Tokyo Olympics in 2021. They stuck together, training long and hard in the men's fours rowing event. And in Paris, they struck gold! It was the first gold in this sport for the US since 1960.

Wrestlemania: American wrestler
Amit Elor won gold in the 68kg freestyle event. At 20, she is the youngest US champion wrestler in Olympic history. With a bronze in the 57kg category, Helen Maroulis earned her third Olympic medal, the most ever by an American woman. She also won gold in 2021 and bronze in 2016.

Great Year!: Scottie Scheffler
was already having one of the best golf seasons ever. He had six PGA Tour wins and had also captured the Masters. With a stunning 62 on the final round at the course outside Paris, he won his first Olympic gold medal, too. Good year all around: Scheffler and his wife, Meredith, had their first child in May! (And while we're on the golf course, congrats to Lydia Ko of New Zealand, who won the women's singles gold.)

American Heroes

Continued from previous page

Faulkner cruised by the Louvre!

Best Yet: When Haley Batten crossed the line in the mountain bike race in second place, her silver medal became the best finish ever by any American in this tough event. Also in cycling, Perris Benegas won silver in the BMX freestyle event.

Watson shouted for his new record!

Super Cyclist: The Olympic cycling road race was long . . . and difficult! Beginning and ending in Paris, racers had to pedal 98 miles through streets, fields, and suburbs. An American woman has not won this race since way back in 1984, but Kristen Faulkner broke that streak, riding to gold past cheering crowds on the streets of Paris!

Almost to the Top: American climber Sam Watson set a world record twice during the speed climbing event. However, he lost in the semifinals. His second record came when he won the bronze medal.

Big Lifts: Hampton Morris weighs 134 pounds. But he is so strong that he can lift 379 pounds over his head! That earned him a bronze in weightlifting, the first by an American since way back in 1984! Then Olivia Reeves won a bronze in the women's 71kg category!

Canada's ❧ Best

Canada won a total of 27 medals, including 9 gold, at the Paris Olympic Games. Here are some of the highlights.

McIntosh had a golden summer!

It Was Summer's Summer Games!:

Swimmer **Summer McIntosh** was the most successful Canadian athlete in Paris. She brought home gold medals in three events: the 200-meter butterfly and the 200- and 400-meter individual medleys. She also earned a silver in the 400-meter freestyle (ahead of **Katie Ledecky**!).

Judo First: **Christa Deguchi** just

missed taking part in the 2021 Tokyo Games. But after a three-year wait, she earned Canada's first-ever judo medal with a gold in the 57kg class.

Rockin' Ruggers: Canada was ahead

of world champion New Zealand at halftime of the women's rugby sevens final. But the Kiwis shut out the Canadians in the second half while scoring twice to win 19-12. Still, a silver was a great result for Canada, which had lost 33-7 to New Zealand in an earlier round and was missing several key players.

Bouncing to a Medal: **Sophiane**

Méthot won the silver in the bouncy, high-flying sport of trampoline gymnastics.

Hammer Time: **Ethan Katzberg** won

the hammer throw, whirling and spinning before launching the heavy iron ball on a long metal wire. **Camryn Rogers** won the women's hammer to complete a big Canadian sweep.

Katzberg goes around and around for gold!

Other Team Sports

WATER POLO: For the first time since 2008, there was a new women's champion. The US had won three straight golds but lost to Australia in Paris after a semifinal penalty shootout. Spain beat Australia in the final. Serbia won its third straight men's gold medal.

VOLLEYBALL: The US women made the indoor final but lost to Italy to win the silver medal. The US men did not do as well, losing in the quarterfinals. Home country France won the men's gold. For the first time ever, no US team won a medal in beach volleyball. Congrats to the men's champs from Sweden and the women's from Brazil.

Denmark and Germany made handball look like fun!

HANDBALL: We hope you got a chance to watch this fast-paced, exciting sport. Why isn't it more popular in the US? It's awesome! Teams of seven players race around a floor about the size of a basketball court. They zing around a small ball and fire it over and over at a goal. But they have to leap into the air to take a shot. We want to play! The women's champ was Norway, who beat France. In the men's tournament, Denmark beat Germany.

FIELD HOCKEY: A double Dutch treat: The Netherlands won both the men's and women's gold medals. Both final games ended in thrilling penalty shootouts!

Individual Highlights

Kayak cross was splashing good fun!

ULTIMATE CHAMP: **Mijaín López Núñez** from Cuba captured his fifth career gold medal in the 130kg Greco-Roman wrestling event. Since the modern Games began in 1896, Lopez became the first five-time gold medalist in an individual event.

TENNIS: In tennis on the red clay of Roland-Garros, **Novak Djokovic** beat **Carlos Alcaraz** in the final to win men's singles. **Zheng Qinwen** won the first tennis gold ever for China in the women's singles.

YOUNG SKATERS: Japan's

Coco Yoshizawa nailed trick after trick to win the women's skateboarding street event. Not bad for a 14-year-old! Australia's **Arisa Trew**, also 14, won the park event.

KAYAK CROSS: This was

a new sport for this Olympics. Four kayakers battled paddle-to-paddle down a whitewater course . . . and even had to flip over once! **Finn Butcher** of New Zealand won the men's gold. **Noemie Fox** of Australia captured the women's event.

FABULOUS FRENCHMAN:

Teddy Riner flipped the No. 1 judoka, **Kim Min-jong** of South Korea, late in their match to win his fourth gold medal in the 100kg category. The French crowd screamed with joy as they watched their countryman win. Later, Riner fought the overtime match in the mixed team event . . . and won again!

FRENCH SWEEP: The only complete medal sweep of the Games came in BMX racing, when three riders from France won all the medals. **Sylvain André** was on top with gold.

Riner (in blue) flipped for gold!

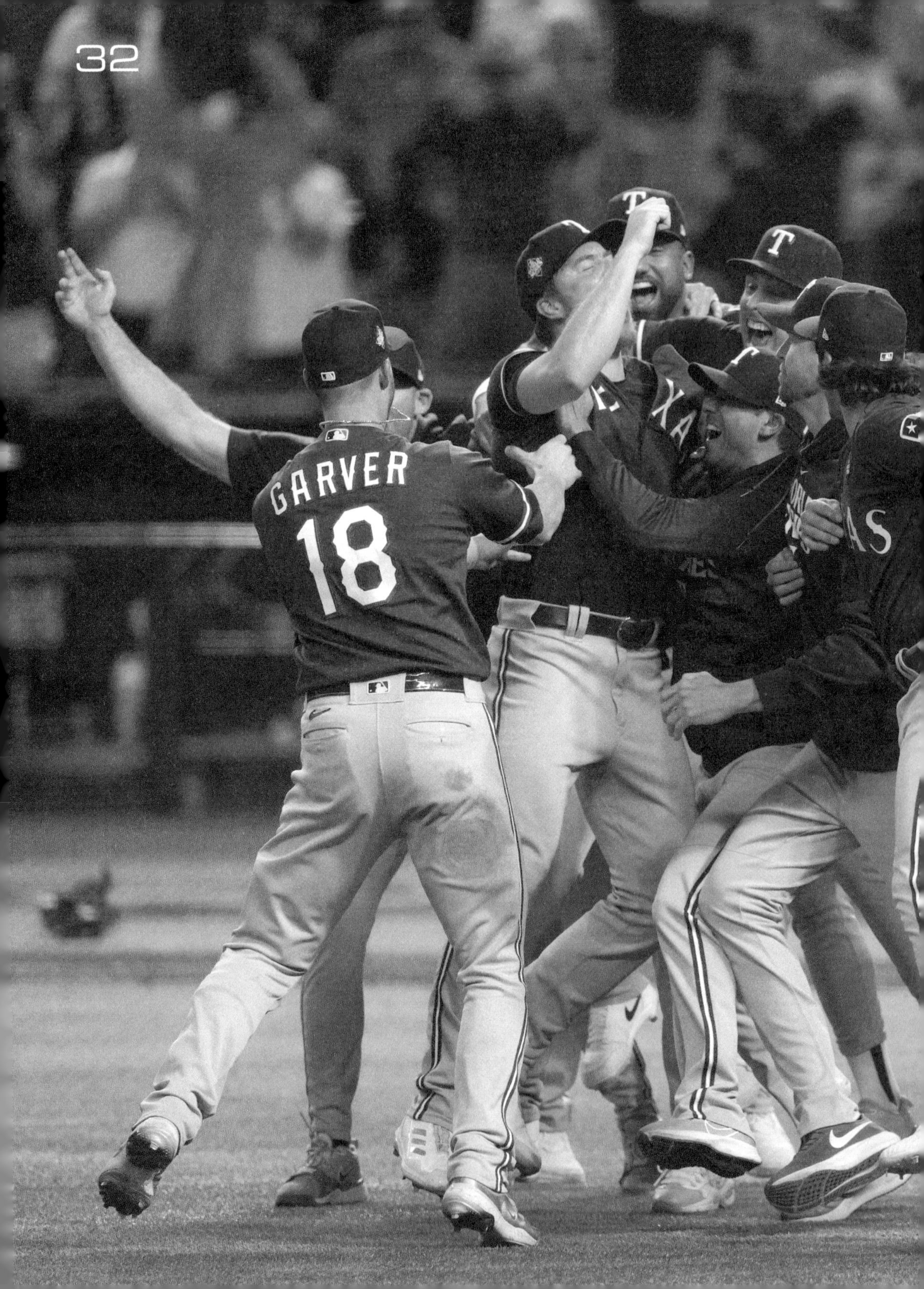
GARVER
18

FINALLY!

The Texas Rangers have been around since 1961. But it took them until 2023 to win their first World Series title. They defeated the Arizona Diamondbacks to set off a Texas-sized celebration. Corey Seager was the MVP, smacking 3 home runs. The series capped off an exciting and record-packed 2023 Major League Baseball season. Read on to make your way around the bases!

MLB

MLB 2023

Baseball was a slightly different sport in 2023. Major League Baseball made a series of rule changes that the league hoped would speed up play. The rules were also supposed to increase steals and hitting. Mission accomplished! The new pitch clock lowered the average game time by 24 minutes to 2 hours and 39 minutes. Steals rose from 2,486 in 2022 to 3,503 in 2023! Batting average and on-base percentages were up, too.

All those new rules attracted lots of fans. Baseball had its highest attendance since 2017, topping more than 70 million people; the nine percent increase from 2022 was the biggest in 30 seasons as well.

Those fans enjoyed some great season-long success stories. The biggest one was the powerhouse offense of the Atlanta Braves. They were led by NL MVP **Ronald Acuña Jr.**, who had a historic year. He was the first player ever with 40 homers and 70 steals in a season. His all-around amazingness was a big reason the Braves became the first team ever with 300-plus homers and 100-plus steals. Their total of 307 homers also tied with the 2019 Minnesota Twins for the most in a season. The Braves were the first team to have four players with at least 35 homers and the first to finish with a team .500 slugging percentage (that's a measure of power hitting).

The big story in the AL was the Baltimore Orioles' comeback. The O's had not made the playoffs since 2016 and had three seasons with 108 or more losses since then. But a nest (get it?) of great young players—including catcher **Adley Rutschman** and 3B/SS **Gunnar Henderson**—ended up with the best record in the league.

Three teams got off to unusual starts. The Tampa Bay Rays were the first team since 2003 to start off 9–0 and outscore their opponents by 50 runs. They won 13 straight

Acuña slides in with one of his MLB-best 73 steals in 2023.

2023 FINAL MLB STANDINGS

AL EAST		AL CENTRAL		AL WEST	
Orioles	101–61	Twins	87–75	Astros	90–72
Rays	99–63	Tigers	78–84	Rangers	90–72
Blue Jays	89–73	Guardians	76–86	Mariners	88–74
Yankees	82–80	White Sox	61–101	Angels	73–89
Red Sox	78–84	Royals	56–106	Athletics	50–112

NL EAST		NL CENTRAL		NL WEST	
Braves	104–58	Brewers	92–70	Dodgers	100–62
Phillies	90–72	Cubs	83–79	Diamondbacks	84–78
Marlins	84–78	Reds	82–80	Padres	82–80
Mets	75–87	Pirates	76–86	Giants	79–83
Nationals	71–91	Cardinals	71–91	Rockies	59–103

before they lost their first game and ended up second to the Orioles with 99 wins. The Pittsburgh Pirates set a team record with 20 wins by May 1. Meanwhile, the St. Louis Cardinals, usually a playoff regular, had their worst start since 1973. When the dust settled in early October, Tampa Bay was in the playoffs, while the Pirates and Cardinals were watching at home!

The final Saturday of the regular season saw five teams clinch playoff spots. The tight NL wild card race ended with the Miami Marlins and Arizona Diamondbacks sliding in ahead of the Chicago Cubs and Cincinnati Reds. It was the Marlins' first playoff appearance in a full season in 20 years! In the AL West, Texas earned a wild card spot but then watched a day later as Houston won the division title. The Toronto Blue Jays held off the Seattle Mariners to earn the final wild card.

While the Los Angeles Angels missed the playoffs again, their megastar DH/P **Shohei Ohtani** continued to stun baseball experts. In his third full season of both pitching and playing DH, Ohtani added new pages to his legend. In one doubleheader, he threw a one-hit shutout in the opener and then hit two homers in the second game!

When the World Series was over, though, an unexpected team ended up as the 2023 champion.

Rutschman's big bat helped a Baltimore breakout.

Around the Bases

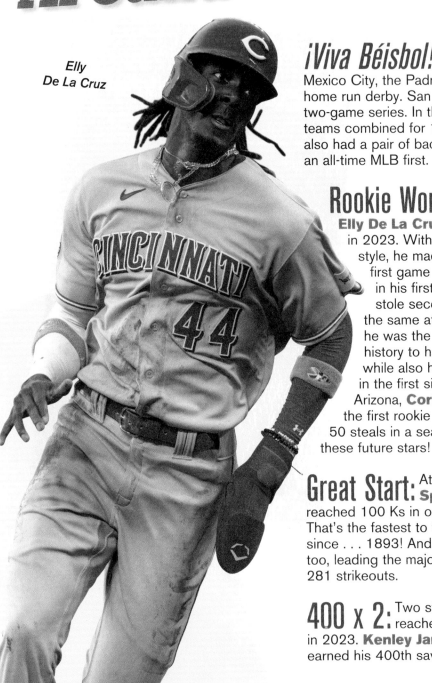

Elly
De La Cruz

¡Viva Béisbol!: In the first MLB games played in Mexico City, the Padres and Giants put on a home run derby. San Diego swept the two-game series. In the first game, the teams combined for 11 homers. Each team also had a pair of back-to-back long balls, an all-time MLB first.

Rookie Wonders: Cincinnati
rookie SS/3B
Elly De La Cruz electrified baseball in 2023. With speed, power, and style, he made headlines from his first game in June. He had 23 hits in his first 16 games and once stole second, third, and home on the same at bat. In his 15th game, he was the first player in baseball history to have a steal and 4 RBI while also hitting for the cycle . . . in the first six innings of a game! In Arizona, **Corbin Carroll** became the first rookie to have 25 homers and 50 steals in a season. Watch out for these future stars!

Great Start: Atlanta's young ace,
Spencer Strider, reached 100 Ks in only 61 innings. That's the fastest to the century mark since . . . 1893! And he had a good finish, too, leading the majors with 20 wins and 281 strikeouts.

400 x 2: Two star closers each
reached the same milestone in 2023. **Kenley Jansen** of the Red Sox earned his 400th save on May 10. Then

Ohtani watches another homer fly out!

first Yankees player with two 3-homer games in a season.

Thanks for the Memories:

Detroit's **Miguel Cabrera** said goodbye to baseball. The future Hall of Famer had 3,174 career hits and 511 homers. He was a two-time MVP and won the Triple Crown in 2012. Cardinals P **Adam Wainwright** retired after 18 seasons and exactly 200 wins. But his last appearance in uniform came as a pinch hitter! The team gave St. Louis fans one more time to cheer for their hero. He struck out, but they didn't care!

Strider had a record-setting beginning.

Craig Kimbrel of the Phillies got No. 400 when he closed out a win on May 26.

Sho-Time:
Angels megastar **Shohei Ohtani** continued to do things no one has ever done. At one point in June, he led the Angels in every offensive category *and* every pitching category (except saves). He wound up atop the AL with 44 homers and was tops in MLB in slugging percentage. An arm injury shortened his pitching season, but he still won 10 games with a 3.14 ERA. It all added up to his second AL MVP trophy!

All Rise!:
Aaron Judge missed part of the season with an injury, but when he was healthy, he was homering! Judge reached 250 career homers faster than any other player. He also became the

MLB 2023 Playoffs

WILD CARD PLAYOFFS

All four Wild Card Playoffs ended in two-game sweeps . . . on the same day! The Diamondbacks came from behind in both games to upset the Brewers. The Phillies started their defense of the NL pennant by whomping the Marlins—**Bryson Stott** had a grand slam in Game 2. In the AL, the Twins won their first playoff series in 21 years, beating the Blue Jays. The Rangers rolled over the Rays, who scored only one run in two games.

ALDS

Rangers 3, Orioles 0

Baltimore came in with the best record in the AL. Texas didn't care. The Rangers smacked around the O's pitching, scoring 21 runs in a shocking three-game sweep.

Astros 3, Twins 1

Houston and Minnesota split the first two games, making this the first playoff series in 2023 in which one team did not win all the games! But Houston then won the next two to reach its seventh-straight ALCS. That's a new AL record! **Yordan Álvarez** had 4 homers for Houston.

NLDS

Phillies 3, Braves 1

Ranger Suárez led a parade of Phillies pitchers that shut down the mighty Braves to win Game 1. Philly won Game 3 and tied a postseason MLB record by hitting 6 homers! Suárez then won Game 4 to clinch the series and the upset.

Diamondbacks 3, Dodgers 0

Arizona pounded Dodgers ace **Clayton Kershaw** on the way to an 11-2 Game 1 win at Dodger Stadium. After winning Game 2 4-2, Arizona hit 4 homers in the third inning of Game 3 (another MLB postseason first) on their way to the shocking sweep. It was the third season in a row that the Dodgers won 100 or more games but lost in the playoffs.

Houston LF Álvarez mashed in the ALDS.

Schwarber smacked homer after homer, but they were not enough to win the NLCS.

NLCS

Diamondbacks 4, Phillies 3

Philly's **Kyle Schwarber** hit the first pitch he saw for a homer . . . and never stopped—but in the end, he wasn't enough. "Schwarbs" finished the series with 5 homers and an amazing OPS of 1.670. The Phillies won Game 1 and Game 2, when Schwarber had 3 homers in those games. Also in Game 2, starter **Aaron Nola** was lights-out and the Phillies won 10-0. But Arizona bounced back with a walk-off Game 3 win, courtesy of **Ketel Marte**'s hit. It won Game 4 by a 6-5 score, thanks to pinch hitter **Alek Thomas**'s dramatic two-run homer and C **Gabriel Moreno**'s go-ahead single in the eighth. Schwarber homered again in a 6-1 Game 5 Phillies win. Down 3–2 in the series, the D-Backs rallied and won Game 6 5-1 behind a great start by **Merrill Kelly**. Game 7 was tight, but Arizona pitching kept the Phillies' big bats mostly quiet. Arizona won 4-2 and reached its second World Series.

ALCS

Rangers 4, Astros 3

Jordan Montgomery led the Rangers to a big Game 1 win with 6.1 innings of shutout pitching. After the Rangers also won Game 2, Houston stormed back with three straight wins, helped by a come-from-behind three-run homer from 2B **José Altuve** to win Game 5. **Adolis García** led the way for Texas in a Game 6 win with a grand slam. In Game 7, García added 2 more homers and 5 RBI as the Rangers headed to their third World Series with an 11-4 win.

García got a celebration ice-cube bath after his Game 1 walk-off homer.

2023 World Series

GAME 1 Texas 6, Arizona 5

After winning the ALCS MVP, **Adolis García** added another page to his memory book. He blasted a walk-off 11th-inning homer to give the Rangers a big first-game win. Texas had tied the game 5-5 in the bottom of the ninth on a two-run homer by SS **Corey Seager**.

GAME 2 Arizona 9, Texas 1

This game was a tale of two pitchers. The Rangers' ace starting pitcher,

Jordan Montgomery, had been great in the playoffs but gave up four runs in six innings in this game. Meanwhile, Arizona's **Merrill Kelly** had another great outing, allowing just one run in seven innings. Arizona DH **Tommy Pham** was the hitting hero, with 4 hits, while D-Backs 2B **Ketel Marte** broke an all-time MLB record with a hit in his 18th-straight postseason game. He also had 2 RBI and **Gabriel Moreno** had a homer as the D-Backs evened the series.

GAME 3 Texas 3, Arizona 1

Seager smacked a two-run homer as the Rangers scored all their runs in the third inning. After Texas starter **Max Scherzer** was injured, **Jon Gray** came on to lead the Rangers staff in shutting down Arizona's bats. Texas also set a single-season record with its ninth-straight postseason win on the road!

GAME 4 Texas 11, Arizona 7

Seager smacked another homer and 2B **Marcus Semien** had 5 RBI as the Rangers put up 10 runs in the first three innings. A homer by C **Jonah Heim** made it 11. The Diamondbacks made things interesting by scoring late, including six runs in the eighth and ninth. But they were in too big a hole; Texas kept its amazing road-game victory streak alive.

GAME 5 Texas 5, Arizona 0

Arizona's **Zac Gallen** threw six nearly perfect innings, but it wasn't enough. The D-Backs were

Marte was a postseason hitting machine.

0 for 9 with runners in scoring position in those innings. Texas finally broke through with a run in the seventh, then added four in the ninth (including a two-run homer by Semien). **Josh Sborz** struck out Marte for the final out, and the Rangers won their first-ever World Series title. The team dates all the way back to 1961!

MVP

Texas SS **Corey Seager** won the Willie Mays World Series MVP Award. Seager had 3 homers in five games and made several great defensive plays. Seager also won the trophy in 2020 with the LA Dodgers, making him only the second position player ever with two World Series MVPs.

2023 MLB Stat Champs

NL Hitting Leaders

54 HOME RUNS
139 RBI
Matt Olson, Braves

.354 BATTING AVERAGE
Luis Arraez, Marlins

217 HITS
73 STOLEN BASES
Ronald Acuña Jr.,
Braves

AL Hitting Leaders

44 HOME RUNS
Shohei Ohtani, Angels

112 RBI
Kyle Tucker, Astros

.330 BATTING AVERAGE
Yandy Díaz, Rays

185 HITS
Marcus Semien, Rangers

NL Pitching Leaders

20 WINS
281 STRIKEOUTS
Spencer Strider, Braves

2.25 ERA
Blake Snell, Padres

39 SAVES
David Bednar, Pirates
Camilo Doval, Giants

AL Pitching Leaders

16 WINS
Chris Bassitt, Blue Jays
Zach Eflin, Rays

2.63 ERA
Gerrit Cole, Yankees

237 STRIKEOUTS
Kevin Gausman, Blue Jays

44 SAVES
Emmanuel Clase,
Guardians

Matt
Olson

2023 MLB Award Winners

Aaron Judge

MOST VALUABLE PLAYER

AL: Shohei Ohtani, Angels
NL: Ronald Acuña Jr., Braves

CY YOUNG AWARD

AL: Gerrit Cole, Yankees
NL: Blake Snell, Padres

HANK AARON AWARD

AL: Shohei Ohtani, Angels
NL: Ronald Acuña Jr., Braves

ROOKIE OF THE YEAR

AL: Gunnar Henderson, Orioles
NL: Corbin Carroll, Diamondbacks

MANAGER OF THE YEAR

AL: Brandon Hyde, Orioles
NL: Skip Schumaker, Marlins

ROBERTO CLEMENTE AWARD

Aaron Judge, Yankees

NFL

THE LAST PASS

Mecole Hardman of the Kansas City Chiefs is just about to catch a pass from Patrick Mahomes (15). When Hardman steps into the end zone, Super Bowl LVIII will be over and the Chiefs will win 25-22 in overtime. Follow the exciting journey from Kickoff Weekend to this pass in the pages ahead!

NFL 2023

The 2023 NFL season included 272 games. Some of them were incredibly exciting, while others were sort of ho-hum. The teams combined for 11,842 points. But after all the dust and confetti settled, the final result was just like the 2022 season: the same team won it all again! But it was a great ride for fans no matter what.

In the NFC, the big story was the rise of the Detroit Lions. Detroit has never won a Super Bowl and had only one playoff win since 1992. Led by QB **Jared Goff** and a powerful defense, the Lions roared to their best record since 1991 and won their first division title since 1993. Though they fell in the playoffs to the San Francisco 49ers, it might be the start of good things in the Motor City.

The Dallas Cowboys were not a surprise, as they won 12 games for the third season in a row. WR **CeeDee Lamb** was a big reason why. He led the NFL with 135 catches and set a Dallas record with 1,749 receiving yards. The 'Boys seemed unstoppable, but lost again in the playoffs, upset by the Green Bay Packers. The Los Angeles Rams were another big NFC story. They were 3–6 at one point, but rallied to win seven of their last eight games. QB **Matthew Stafford** was outstanding, with 16 TD passes in that eight-game stretch. He had a lot of help from WR **Puka Nacua**, who shocked many fans by setting all-time single-season rookie records with 105 catches for 1,486 yards.

In the AFC, the Baltimore Ravens had a great streak of their own, winning 10 of 11 games midseason to wind up atop the conference. They were led by NFL MVP QB **Lamar Jackson**'s multi-talented attack.

CeeDee Lamb

Stroud was a standout for Houston.

66

That's how many different players started at least one game at quarterback in 2023, tying an all-time record. Ten of them were rookies, the most in a season since 1950.

The Ravens D also gave up the fewest points in the league. The Houston Texans were a surprise division champ, led by rookie QB **C.J. Stroud**. He finished second all-time among rookies with 4,108 passing yards, and his 470-yard performance in a win over Tampa Bay was also a rookie best.

On the other end of the age scale, 38-year-old QB **Joe Flacco** started five games for the Cleveland Browns. He won four to send them into the playoffs!

The 2023 season also was the last for New England Patriots head coach **Bill Belichick**. He left the job with a record six Super Bowl titles along with 31 playoff victories, also the most ever.

As for the repeat NFL champ? Read on to find out how they got there!

2023 Final Regular-Season Standings

AFC EAST		AFC NORTH		AFC SOUTH		AFC WEST	
Bills*	11–6	Ravens*	13–4	Texans*	10–7	Chiefs*	11–6
Dolphins*	11–6	Browns*	11–6	Jaguars	9–8	Raiders	8–9
Jets	7–10	Steelers*	10–7	Colts	9–8	Broncos	8–9
Patriots	4–13	Bengals	9–8	Titans	6–11	Chargers	5–12

NFC EAST		NFC NORTH		NFC SOUTH		NFC WEST	
Cowboys*	12–5	Lions*	12–5	Buccaneers*	9–8	49ers*	12–5
Eagles*	11–6	Packers*	9–8	Saints	9–8	Rams*	10–7
Giants	6–11	Vikings	7–10	Falcons	7–10	Seahawks	9–8
Commanders	4–13	Bears	7–10	Panthers	2–15	Cardinals	4–13

*Playoff Team

Weeks 1-4

What a dive! Barkley barely squeaked in for a Week 2 TD.

Browns Bounce:

Cincinnati Bengals QB **Joe Burrow** signed the biggest contract in NFL history shortly before this matchup. Then he went out and played one of his worst games, a career-low 82 passing yards. Cleveland's **Deshaun Watson** threw a TD pass and ran for another as the Browns won easily 24-3.

WEEK 2

A Giant Comeback:

The NY Giants did something they had not done since 1949—they came back from 21 points down! Against the Arizona Cardinals, RB **Saquon Barkley** scored 2 TDs in the second half. Then **Graham Gano** kicked a 34-yard field goal for the winning points in the 31-28 game.

All Allen: Buffalo QB **Josh Allen** had a terrible first game, with 4 turnovers. He made up for it in a Week 2 38-10 win over the Las Vegas Raiders. Allen tossed 3 TDs and had 274 yards passing . . . and no interceptions! He also set a career record by completing his first 13 passes in a row.

Whew!: Washington moved to 2–0 for the first time since 2011 by shutting down the Denver Broncos' two-point attempt at the end of the game. The Commanders had come back from 18 points, but Denver scored late. The Washington D broke up a two-point pass to hold on for a 35-33 win.

WEEK 1

Lions Roar: Detroit got the season off to a big start by surprising the defending-champion Kansas City Chiefs 21-20. The Detroit D allowed only two field goals in the second half to the powerful KC offense. A 50-yard pick-six by Detroit's **Brian Branch** was the key play of the game.

Aaron's Short Season: Superstar QB **Aaron Rodgers** was injured on his fourth play with his new team, the Jets. A torn Achilles tendon ended his season much, much earlier than he and Jets fans wanted. New York did go on to upset the Buffalo Bills 22-16. **Xavier Gipson** returned a punt 65 yards in overtime for the walk-off win.

WEEK 3

Pile o' Points!: The Dolphins swam right over the Broncos, winning 70-20. Miami's score tied the second-most points ever scored in an NFL game. Their 726 total yards were second-most, too. They became the only NFL team with 350 yards both passing and running. Rookie **De'Von Achane** led the way with 203 yards rushing and 2 TDs. RB **Raheem Mostert** had 4 TDs, while QB **Tua Tagovailoa** threw 4 TD passes. The 70 points were the most since Washington scored 72 points in a game way back in 1966!

Record Kicker: Colts K **Matt Gay** booted four field goals of 50 or more yards, a new NFL record for a single game. The final one was the most important. He drilled a 53-yarder in overtime to give his team a 22-19 win over the Ravens.

Taylor in the House!: Singing superstar **Taylor Swift** was a guest of Chiefs TE Travis Kelce at his team's game against the Bears. Swift joined a stadium full of Chiefs fans watching their team dismantle the Bears 41-10. Kelce caught one of **Patrick Mahomes**' 3 TD passes.

Dallas Downer: After winning its first two games, Dallas hit a roadblock against Arizona. QB **Joshua Dobbs** won his first NFL game and **Matt Prater** made a 62-yard field goal and Arizona won 28-16.

Love the Comeback: The Packers trailed the Saints 17-0 in the fourth quarter, but QB **Jordan Love** led a great comeback. Green Bay scored the final 18 points of the game, capped off by a TD catch by **Romeo Doubs**, to win 18-17.

WEEK 4

Loud Stroud: The Houston Texans whomped the Pittsburgh Steelers 30-6 as Houston rookie QB **C.J. Stroud** continued a great start. He had 306 passing yards and 2 TDs. Stroud had the second-most passing yards by any player in his first four NFL games . . . ever! He also had not thrown a pick yet!

Sizzling San Fran: The 49ers won their fourth straight as RB **Christian McCaffrey** scored 4 TDs. QB **Brock Purdy** added TDs on the ground and through the air as the Niners beat the Arizona Cardinals 35-16, making it nine straight regular-season wins to start his NFL career.

McCaffrey had 4 TDs in Week 4!

Weeks 5-8

WEEK 5

More Moore: The Chicago Bears won their first game of the season, beating Washington 40-20. WR **D.J. Moore** was the big star, catching 8 passes for an incredible 230 yards and 3 TDs. QB **Justin Fields** had a total of 4 TD tosses. The Bears also broke a losing streak of 14 games dating back to 2022.

Purdy Good: San Francisco tied its all-time best winning streak at 15 when the 49ers rode all over the Cowboys 42-10. The SF D picked off Dallas QB **Dak Prescott** three times and had 4 sacks. SF QB **Brock Purdy** had one of his best games, throwing 4 TD passes, including 3 to TE **George Kittle** (on Kittle's only three catches of the game!).

Bengals Chase a Win: Cincinnati defeated Arizona 34-20. **Ja'Marr Chase** had his best NFL game, making 15 catches for 192 yards and 3 TDs. The 15 grabs were the most ever by a Bengals receiver.

Loving London: Jacksonville and Buffalo traveled to London, England, for a game at Tottenham Stadium. The Jaguars' long flight home was the happier one, as they upset the Bills 25-20. RB **Travis Etienne** led the way with 136 yards on the ground and a pair of TDs.

Patriots Pounded: The glory days of **Tom Brady**-less Pats are definitely over. New England lost 34-0 to the Saints; it was their second-worst shutout loss at home in team history. A week earlier, they had lost 38-3 to Dallas in longtime coach **Bill Belichick**'s worst-ever defeat. It was a long season in New England.

WEEK 6

No More No Loss: The NFL's final pair of undefeated teams lost on the same day in big upsets. The 49ers fell to Cleveland 19-17, missing a game-winning field goal at the end. Injuries to big stars RB **Christian McCaffrey** and WR **Deebo Samuel** hurt the Niners. Meanwhile, the Eagles were shocked by the Jets, whose defense continued to shine. The Jets picked off 3 passes by Philly QB **Jalen Hurts** and won 20-14. It was the Jets' first win ever

Chase chased down a Bengals record.

against the Eagles—they had been 0–12!

Bills Escape:
Buffalo had only one loss, but nearly got another against the feisty Giants. The Bills had been rolling, but their offense was not clicking against New York's D. The Bills did not score until the fourth quarter but won 14-9. The Giants almost pulled out a miracle, but a final pass from the 1-yard line fell incomplete.

Leapin' Lions!:
Detroit continued a strong start to the season, moving to 5–1 with a 20-6 win over Tampa Bay. QB **Jared Goff** had 353 passing yards and 2 TDs to lead the way. He needed to work hard after Detroit lost its two starting RBs to injuries. But they won to stay in first place in the NFC North.

WEEK 7

Pats Power:
Coach **Bill Belichick** of the Patriots won his 300th career game in surprising fashion. New England came in as big underdogs to the powerful Bills but won 29-25 on a late TD. **Mac Jones** tossed a 1-yard score to TE **Mike Gesicki** for the upset. The Pats' D was all over Bills QB **Josh Allen**.

Tyson Who?:
An undrafted rookie named **Tyson Bagent** led the Bears to a surprise win over the Raiders. Starting in place of star **Justin Fields**, Bagent was

Will Levis

excellent, completing 21 passes including 1 TD. He got help from RB **D'Onta Foreman**, who scored twice in the 30-12 win.

Power Matchup:
In a battle of 5-1 teams, the Eagles showed that they had the upper hand . . . for now. They knocked off Miami 31-17. Philly QB **Jalen Hurts** had a great game, throwing 2 TD passes and running for another score. WR **A.J. Brown** had 10 catches for 137 yards as the Eagles moved to the top of the NFC.

WEEK 8

Denver Surprise:
The Broncos forced 5 turnovers and upset the Chiefs 24-9. Denver QB **Russell Wilson** had 3 TD passes, while his defensive teammates shut down KC QB **Patrick Mahomes**.

Will the Thrill:
Tennessee started a rookie QB, **Will Levis**, and he had a game to remember. He became only the third player ever with 4 TD passes in his first NFL game. He got most of the help from veteran WR **DeAndre Hopkins**, who caught 3 of the scoring passes as the Titans beat the Falcons 28-23.

Good Company:
Chargers QB **Justin Herbert** had 3 TD passes—and no interceptions—to lead his team to a 30-13 win over the Bears. Star RB **Austin Ekeler** had 94 receiving yards and a TD.

Weeks 9-12

WEEK 9

Rookie Magic: Houston fell behind Tampa Bay with 46 seconds left. No problem, said Texans rookie QB **C.J. Stroud**. He led his team to the game-winning score, hitting **Tank Dell** with a TD pass with six seconds left to win 39-37. Stroud's 470 passing yards were the most ever in a game by a rookie; his 5 TD passes also tied a rookie record. A huge play in the game was a field goal by **Dare Ogunbowale**. Why so big? Because he's a running back! He had to step in when the Texans' kicker was hurt; the runner-turned-kicker made a key 29-yard three-pointer!

Beckham made it back to the end zone.

Third Team's the Charm: QB **Joshua Dobbs** began the season in Arizona. Then he was traded to Atlanta. Then he was sent to Minnesota. Four days after joining the Vikings, he began their game with the Falcons as the backup. But when starter **Jaren Hall** was hurt, Dobbs—with almost no practice time—led them to a game-winning score with 22 seconds left to beat the Falcons 31-28.

Here Come the Ravens: Baltimore moved to 7–2 on the season with a big 37-3 win over Seattle. WR **Odell Beckham Jr.**, once a superstar, caught his first TD since 2021, and **Gus Edwards** had 2 rushing scores. The Ravens defense continued to be great—this was its fourth game giving up 9 or fewer points!

WEEK 10

Brownout in Baltimore: The Browns rallied from 14 points behind to upset the Ravens in Baltimore. The Ravens led 31-17 in the fourth quarter, but Cleveland QB **Deshaun Watson** threw a TD pass and the Browns' D scored a pick-six. The extra point was missed, but K **Dustin Hopkins** got another chance on the game's final play. His 40-yard field goal made it 33-31 Browns.

Seahawks Fly: Seattle got a last-play field goal of its own from **Jason Myers** to edge the Commanders 29-26. QB **Geno Smith** set up Myers' game-winner with 2 long passes with less than a minute left.

Philly's Hurts led the way in a Super Bowl rematch.

Tommy Who?: Tommy **DeVito**, a third-string backup QB, led the Giants to a 31-19 win over the Commanders. DeVito became only the fourth Giants rookie to throw at least 3 TD passes. Washington didn't help itself with 6 turnovers, including 3 interceptions by QB **Sam Howell**.

Fly Eagles Fly: It was a Super Bowl rematch. The Chiefs beat the Eagles last season; this time, it was Philly that came out on top 21-17. Philly QB **Jalen Hurts** hit **DeVonta Smith** with a long pass to set up Hurts' second rushing TD of the game and take the lead. Kansas City receivers dropped two throws by QB **Patrick Mahomes** and the Chiefs' comeback fell short. Still, both teams were on track for deep playoff runs . . . and maybe another matchup!

Offensive Showdown: The Lions also got a game-winner from their kicker, **Riley Patterson**. Detroit and San Diego piled on the offense, scoring 38 points each before Patterson's kick made the final score 41-38 Detroit. San Diego QB **Justin Herbert** had 4 TDs, while Detroit's **Jared Goff** had 2. Detroit star RB **David Montgomery** helped with a 75-yard TD run.

One Too Many: The Bills thought they had escaped an upset against the Broncos. Denver K **Wil Lutz** had missed a very late field goal. But wait! Buffalo had 12 defenders on the field and earned a penalty (that's one too many players, of course). Lutz made his do-over kick, and Denver won 24-22.

WEEK 11

Defense = Offense: A pick-six is one of football's most game-changing plays. In the Cowboys' 33-10 win over the Panthers, **DaRon Bland** showed why. He snagged an interception, did a somersault, and then got up to race to the end zone. Bland tied an NFL record with his fourth pick-six of the season.

WEEK 12

Pick-6 x 5: The Cowboys' Bland had yet another pick-six, setting a new NFL season record of five. Dallas piled up the yards and points against Washington and won 45-10. QB **Dak Prescott** had 4 TD passes to four different receivers as the Cowboys kept up a solid 2023 season.

Bengals Miss Burrow: Losing your star QB for the season makes things tough. That's what happened to the Bengals when **Joe Burrow** hurt his wrist. Pittsburgh took advantage, holding Cincinnati to only 222 yards on offense in a 16-10 win. Meanwhile, RB **Najee Harris** ran for 99 yards and a score and TE **Pat Freiermuth** had 120 yards receiving for the Steelers.

Weeks 13-16

WEEK 13

Purdy Good!: The 49ers moved to the top of the NFC with a big 42-19 win over the Eagles in Philadelphia. In the matchup of last season's NFC Championship Game, the Niners scored TDs on six possessions in a row. WR **Deebo Samuel** led the way with 3 of those scores.

Super Cheetah:

Miami's speedy WR **Tyreek "Cheetah" Hill** continued to dominate defenses. He had TD catches that went for 78 and 60 yards, adding to his league-best 12 receiving scores. Miami's defense also had a pick-six on the way to a big 45-15 win over Washington.

TE Day in New Orleans:

Detroit TE **Sam LaPorta** had the best game of his career, with 9 catches for 140 yards. One of them was good for a TD to help the Lions beat the Saints 33-28. The victory moved Detroit to 9–3, the first time they had achieved that record since way back in 1962!

WEEK 14

Cincy Surprise: When the Bengals lost star QB **Joe Burrow**, some folks might have thought the team was done. But rookie QB **Jake Browning** surprised them! In Week 14, he led his team to their second straight win, a 34-14 pounding of the Colts. Browning had 2 more TD passes and ran for a score as well.

Old Guy Wins!: Cleveland stayed in the playoff hunt when it got a win from its fourth different QB this season. Veteran **Joe Flacco**, 38 years old, stepped in to throw 3 TD passes as the Browns beat the Jaguars 31-27.

Tough Call: The Chiefs trailed the Bills 20-17 late in the fourth quarter. Then they pulled off a miracle—a pass to **Travis Kelce**, who passed backward to **Kadarius Toney**, who ran in for what would have been a game-winner. Oops! Toney lined up offsides on the play, and it was called back. The Chiefs were upset about the penalty, but it stood, as did the Bills win.

Runnin' Raven: For only the fourth time in NFL history (but the second time this season!), a game ended on a punt-return TD. The Rams tied the Ravens on a field goal with seven seconds left, to force overtime. The Rams got the ball first, but

Sam LaPorta

Wallace celebrated with an end zone flip!

had to punt. Baltimore's **Tylan Wallace** returned the ball 76 yards to give his team a shocking 37-31 win.

WEEK 15

Turnaround City: In Week 14, the
Raiders lost 3-0 to the Vikings. On Thursday night of Week 15, Las Vegas shocked the NFL by setting a team record for points when they beat the Chargers 63-21. Eight different Raiders scored TDs in the rout, the most by a team in a game since 1950.

Ravens Clinch: With a 23-7 win over
the Jaguars, the Ravens sealed up a playoff spot. They can thank amazing QB **Lamar Jackson**. He made the play of the game by spinning away from a tackler, scrambling, and then hitting TE **Isaiah Likely** with a key TD pass. At 11–3, Baltimore had the AFC's best record.

Suddenly Seattle: The Seahawks
capped off Week 15 with a thrilling 20-17 win over the Eagles. QB **Drew Lock** hit **Jaxon Smith-Njigba** with a TD pass with just 28 seconds left to thrill the hometown Seattle fans. The loss put Philly behind Dallas in the NFC East, while also keeping Seattle's playoff chances alive.

Big Bills: Buffalo continued its late
charge for a playoff spot, trouncing Dallas 31-10. RB **James Cook** led the way, setting a career record with 179 rushing yards; he also scored a pair of TDs. Dallas had come into the game at 10–3 and on a five-game winning streak.

WEEK 16

Here Come the Rams: At one
point, the Rams were 3–6 and looking at another losing season. But QB **Matthew Stafford** led a big turnaround. LA made it five wins in six games with a 30-22 win over the Saints. Rookie WR **Puka Nacua** continued to amaze, with a TD and a career-high 164 receiving yards. He was close to the NFL rookie yardage record!

Lions Clinch: For the first time since
1993, the Lions were division champs. They clinched the historic NFC North title with a 30-24 win over the Vikings. A last-minute interception near the goal line by **Ifeatu Melifonwu** sealed the big W.

Amazing Amari: Cleveland WR
Amari Cooper set a team record with 265 receiving yards to lead his team to a big 36-22 win over Houston. Cooper had 2 TD catches and also scored a two-point conversion. Though **Joe Flacco** is the Browns' fourth QB of the season, the team looked good for a playoff spot.

14 in 7: The Raiders shocked the
Chiefs in Kansas City with a 20-14 win thanks to two big defensive plays. In the space of *seven* seconds of game time, the Raiders returned a fumble AND an interception for touchdowns. It was a big day for the Raiders D overall, holding the powerful Chiefs offense in check for the upset.

Weeks 17-18

WEEK 17

Ravens Fly High: Baltimore set itself up as the top team heading into the playoffs with a 56-19 win over Miami. The win gave Baltimore a two-game lead over Miami, and the Ravens showed they were a Super Bowl favorite. QB **Lamar Jackson** threw for 321 yards and 5 TDs, including 2 to **Isaiah Likely**. Baltimore clinched the AFC No. 1 seed.

Thank You, Pittsburgh!: That's what the LA Rams were saying after the Steelers beat the Seahawks 30-23. The Rams had already squeaked out a win over the Giants 26-25 (New York missed a game-winning field goal attempt). The Pittsburgh W meant that the Rams clinched the No. 6 seed in the playoffs!

WEEK 18

Jags Sag: A win over the Titans would send the Jaguars to the playoffs. But Jacksonville could not pull it off, and Tennessee won 28-20. QB **Trevor Lawrence** just missed scoring a tying TD on a fourth-quarter goal-line dive. The Jags loss clinched playoff spots for the Steelers and Bills in the AFC.

Texans Triumph: Meanwhile, Houston had beaten Indianapolis a day before. Their 23-19 win clinched a playoff spot. The Texans then watched on TV as the Jaguars lost, making the Texans and standout rookie QB **C.J. Stroud** the AFC South champs!

Puka Nacua

NFC All Set: In the NFC, Tampa Bay beat Carolina 9-0 in a defensive battle. But it was enough to give the Bucs their third NFC South title in a row. In the NFC North, the Packers beat the Bears 17-9 thanks to 2 **Jordan Love** TD passes. The win sent the Pack to the playoffs as a wild card.

Record Setter: As the Rams beat the 49ers 21-20, WR **Puka Nacua** wrapped up all-time NFL rookie season records with 105 catches and 1,486 receiving yards.

Wild-Card Playoffs

AFC

Texans 45, Browns 14

C.J. Stroud continued his awesome season with a rookie record-tying 3 TD passes in the Texans' rout of the Browns. The Houston D was huge, too, allowing only 2 **Joe Flacco** TD passes. At 22, Stroud was also the youngest QB to win a playoff game.

Chiefs 26, Dolphins 7

It was minus-four degrees at kickoff, the fourth-coldest game in NFL history. But the Chiefs warmed up quickly, piling on points while their fans piled on layers of clothing! WR **Rashee Rice** starred for KC, catching 8 passes for 130 yards and a TD.

Bills 31, Steelers 17

Buffalo got so much snow that this game had to be moved a day forward. Fans were hired to clear the huge snowdrifts from the seats before the game! Buffalo QB **Josh Allen** had no trouble with the cold and snow. He had 3 TD passes and ran 52 yards for another TD.

NFC

Packers 48, Cowboys 32

The biggest shock of this round was the Packers' big win over the Cowboys . . . *in Dallas!* Green Bay QB **Jordan Love** threw 3 TD passes, and RB **Aaron Jones** ran for 3 more.

Lions 24, Rams 23

Detroit QB **Jared Goff** got a bit of revenge on his old team, while also beating the player who took his place, former Detroit QB **Matthew Stafford**. LA's **Puka Nacua** ended his amazing season with a single-game playoff rookie record 181 yards receiving, but they were not enough. Detroit held LA to field goals in two late drives to preserve the win.

Buccaneers 32, Eagles 9

What happened to the Eagles? They were 10–1 at one point, but then lost five of their last six regular-season games. Their sudden sad streak continued in this game, which Tampa won thanks to QB **Baker Mayfield**'s 3 TD passes.

Green Bay "Loved" what their QB did to Dallas!

Goff put the Lions one step away from the Super Bowl.

Divisional Playoffs

AFC

Ravens 34, Texans 10

The Ravens' defense held the Texans' offense to only a field goal (Houston got a punt-return TD). Meanwhile, **Lamar Jackson** did what he almost always does—dominate. He scored 2 rushing TDs, while throwing for 2 more scores to lead the No. 1 seed to the AFC title game.

Chiefs 27, Bills 24

Bills K **Tyler Bass** missed a game-tying 44-yard field goal and the Chiefs held on to win. **Patrick Mahomes** was his usual excellent self, throwing 2 TD passes to TE **Travis Kelce** (as Kelce's girlfriend Taylor Swift watched). Bills QB **Josh Allen** ran for 2 TDs, but it was not enough. The Chiefs headed to their sixth straight AFC Championship Game.

NFC

49ers 24, Packers 21

The Packers nearly pulled off a big upset. But they were stopped on fourth down early and missed a field goal late. The 49ers had to come from behind in the fourth quarter, finally clinching the win on **Christian McCaffrey**'s second TD run of the day. The Niners also picked off 2 **Jordan Love** passes. It will be San Fran's fourth NFC Championship Game spot in five seasons.

Lions 31, Bucs 23

Bucs QB **Baker Mayfield** had 3 TD passes for Tampa Bay, but Lions QB **Jared Goff** was excellent as well. He had 2 TD throws and led several long scoring drives. The Lions headed to the NFC title game for the first time since 1991.

Conference Championships

Aiyuk made this key circus catch for SF.

49ers 34, Lions 31

The Lions thought they might have their first Super Bowl trip in the bag. They led the 49ers 24-7 at halftime. San Francisco had not been able to move the ball, and Detroit was flying high. But the Niners rallied with a huge second half to disappoint Detroit fans. SF QB **Brock Purdy** was electric, making pinpoint passes and finding space for key runs. With TD runs from **Christian McCaffrey** and **Elijah Mitchell** and a TD catch by **Brandon Aiyuk**, the Niners scored 27 points in a row. Detroit QB **Jared Goff** had a late TD, but there was not enough time for more. San Francisco earned its eighth NFC title.

Chiefs 17, Ravens 10

Lamar Jackson might have won MVP (page 62), but he was far from the best player in this game. The Ravens' QB did not play very well, while Kansas City's amazing **Patrick Mahomes** was on fire. Scrambling, finding open receivers, flipping passes every which way . . . Mahomes did more than enough to get the Chiefs the points they needed. TE **Travis Kelce** helped a lot, catching 11 passes for 116 yards and a TD. He became the NFL's all-time leader in career playoff catches, too! KC headed to its fourth Super Bowl in five seasons!

Travis Kelce

Back-to-Back

SUPER BOWL LVIII

McCaffrey scored a key early TD.

Neither team scored in the first quarter, though the 49ers moved the ball well. They opened the scoring early in the second on a **Jake Moody** field goal. It went 55 yards, setting a new all-time Super Bowl record. After the Chiefs fumbled, the Niners drove down and scored the game's first TD on a trick play. WR **Jauan Jennings** caught a backward pass from QB **Brock Purdy**. Then Jennings threw back across the field to RB **Christian McCaffrey**, who ran in for the score. Kansas City did get a field goal to make the halftime score 10-3.

In the second half, the 49ers continued to bottle up the Chiefs offense, including picking off a pass by Mahomes. But the Niners

The first three quarters of Super Bowl LVIII in Las Vegas were anything but super. The San Francisco 49ers and Kansas City Chiefs were both sloppy, combining for 4 turnovers, 12 penalties, and 10 punts. But a thrilling, back-and-forth fourth quarter and dramatic overtime made up for all that. Led by the incredible **Patrick Mahomes**, the Chiefs won 25-22 in a rematch of the Super Bowl for the 2020 season. The victory made KC the first back-to-back NFL champs since 2004.

Kelce and Swift at the center of it all

offense couldn't score, and KC got a new Super Bowl–record field goal, 57 yards by **Harrison Butker**. Then the Niners made a huge mistake. A punt by KC hit a Niners defender; the Chiefs recovered at the 16-yard line. Mahomes threw a go-ahead TD pass to **Marquez Valdes-Scantling**: KC 16-SF 13.

After a clutch fourth-down play to keep the chains moving in the fourth quarter, Purdy threw a TD pass of his own to Jennings. The Niners were ahead! But they missed the extra point, so it was 19-16 Niners.

Back came the Chiefs. Star TE **Travis Kelce** had only 1 receiving yard in the first half. In the second, he showed his skills, catching 8 passes for 92 yards. Many came on a key drive that tied the score at 19-19 on another Butker FG. Moody then put SF up 22-19 with a strong 53-yard kick.

Mahomes had less than two minutes left, but he worked his usual magic and led the Chiefs to a field goal that tied the game 22-22 with just three seconds left. For only the second time ever, the Super Bowl headed to overtime!

San Francisco got the ball first and drove to another field goal. Then it was Mahomes' turn, and he did it again! Mixing passes and runs, and scrambling for a key first down himself, Mahomes took the Chiefs to the 3-yard line. With everyone on their feet in Vegas and at home, he hit **Mecole Hardman** for the game-winning score!

A Special Group

These are the only QBs to win three or more Super Bowls. Only Brady, at age 27, was younger than Mahomes, who was 28 when he won his third.

Tom Brady, 7
Terry Bradshaw, 4
Joe Montana, 4
Troy Aikman, 3
Patrick Mahomes, 3

2023 NFL Awards

MOST VALUABLE PLAYER

LAMAR JACKSON
RAVENS

OFFENSIVE PLAYER OF THE YEAR

CHRISTIAN McCAFFREY
49ERS

DEFENSIVE PLAYER OF THE YEAR

MYLES GARRETT
BROWNS

OFFENSIVE ROOKIE OF THE YEAR

C.J. STROUD
TEXANS

DEFENSIVE ROOKIE OF THE YEAR

WILL ANDERSON JR.
TEXANS

COMEBACK PLAYER OF THE YEAR

JOE FLACCO
BROWNS

COACH OF THE YEAR

KEVIN STEFANSKI
BROWNS

WALTER PAYTON NFL MAN OF THE YEAR

CAMERON HEYWARD
STEELERS

Lamar Jackson

2023 NFL Stats Leaders

36 TD PASSES
Dak Prescott, Cowboys

4,624 PASSING YARDS
Tua Tagovailoa, Dolphins

1,459 RUSHING YARDS
Christian McCaffrey, 49ers

18 RUSHING TDS
Raheem Mostert, Dolphins

135 CATCHES
CeeDee Lamb, Cowboys

1,749 RECEIVING YARDS
Tyreek Hill, Dolphins

13 TD CATCHES
Mike Evans, Buccaneers
Tyreek Hill, Dolphins

36 FIELD GOALS
Brandon Aubrey, Cowboys

9 INTERCEPTIONS
DaRon Bland, Cowboys

19 SACKS
T.J. Watt, Steelers

183 TOTAL TACKLES
Bobby Wagner, Seahawks

Tyreek Hill

2024 HALL OF FAME CLASS

Welcome seven new members to the Pro Football Hall of Fame in Canton, Ohio. They got the call during Super Bowl week and were inducted in an August ceremony. Five were defensive stars, one was a top WR, while the seventh was perhaps the best return man ever!

Dwight Freeney, DE
Dominant pass rusher with 125.5 career sacks, most with the Colts in the early 2000s.

Randy Gradishar, LB
Heart of Broncos' great 1970s defense, seven Pro Bowls in 10 seasons, plus 1978 Defensive Player of the Year.

Devin Hester, KR ▶▶▶
Scored an NFL-record 19 touchdowns on punt or kickoff

returns, all but one with the Chicago Bears; also returned a kick for a TD in Super Bowl XLI.

◀◀◀ Andre Johnson, WR
Texans' top WR all-time, with seven 1,000-yard seasons, twice leading NFL, and earning seven Pro Bowl spots.

Steve McMichael, DT
Heart of the Bears' awesome 1980s defense that helped them win Super Bowl XX. Nicknamed Mongo, his 95 sacks were third most by a DT all-time.

2023 FANTASY STARS

Some fantasy superstars had quiet years because of injury (**Justin Jefferson Joe Burrow**), but other, less-famous players became great ways to pile up points (**Breece Hall, Puka Nacua**). How did your team do? Here are the top scorers in fantasy football recorded on NFL.com.

POSITION/PLAYER/POINTS

QB	**Josh Allen**	392.64 ▶
RB	**Christian McCaffrey**	391.30
WR	**CeeDee Lamb**	403.20
TE	**Sam LaPorta**	239.30
K	**Brandon Aubrey**	177.00
DEF	**Baltimore Ravens**	174.00

◀◀◀ Julius Peppers, DE

2002 Defensive Rookie of the Year Award winner kicked off 17-year career that ended with 159.5 sacks, fourth-most all-time, plus nine Pro Bowl spots.

Patrick Willis, LB

2007 DROY after leading NFL with 174 tackles; led again in 2009. Named to Pro Bowl in seven of eight seasons.

WHY CANTON?

So why do football's legends live in this small Ohio city? Because that is where the league was formed in 1920. **TRIVIA TIME:** For its first two seasons, it was known as the American Pro Football Association (APFA).

COLLEGE FOOTBALL

HAIL TO THE VICTORS!

Those words are from Michigan's fight song . . . and it's what came true when the Wolverines won the College Football Playoff for the first time. Led by QB J.J. McCarthy (with trophy), Michigan beat a very strong Washington team 34-13 to set off a big celebration. For a look back at that game and at the whole 2023 college football season, turn the page!

College Football 2023

College football made lots of news on the field in 2023. Touchdowns were scored, sacks were made, bowl games were played, a champion was crowned (in early 2024, of course). But the sport made even more news off the field. By the time you read this, the 2024 season will almost be over, with lots of teams playing in different conferences. The moves reshaped college football.

The shakeup started in June 2023 when USC and UCLA left the Pac-12 to jump to the Big Ten. (Of course that name doesn't mean much: the Big Ten now has 18 teams!) The remaining 10 teams in the Pac-12 could not get a big enough TV deal, so other schools soon started jumping out.

In August, Oregon and Washington also joined the Big Ten. Colorado then moved to the Big 12, and Utah, Arizona, and Arizona State followed soon after. That left just four teams in the Pac-12 (and 16 in the Big "12"!). California and Stanford switched to the ACC, leaving poor Oregon State and Washington State

*Florida State's
Jordan Travis*

as the "Pac-2." (They'll both play some Mountain West teams in 2024.) It was a sudden, sad ending for a conference that began way back in 1915. It also meant that there are now four "power" conferences in college football for 2024 and beyond.

But what about the news on the field in 2023? A lot of familiar teams were in the mix for the four-team College Football Playoff. Michigan dominated the Big Ten, while Washington romped through the final season of the Pac-12. Texas was a bit of a surprise in the Southwest Conference. In the SEC, it came down to the conference title game, where Alabama beat undefeated

After 10 teams left, 2023 was the last for the Pac-12.

Georgia, preventing the Bulldogs from trying for three national titles in a row.

Florida State was the biggest surprise of the season. The Seminoles started out unranked but ended the pre-bowl season undefeated and ranked No. 5. However, they lost their two top QBs. Without them, the team was left out of the Playoff by the selection committee. It caused a lot of uproar—an undefeated team missing the Playoff? But the committee ended up looking good when FSU was swamped in the Orange Bowl by Georgia (page 77).

In the end, the top four teams gave fans a pair of great semifinals, and a final that made one of the most famous football schools in the nation into the champion.

FINAL TOP 10

1. **Michigan**
2. **Washington**
3. **Texas**
4. **Georgia**
5. **Alabama**
6T. **Oregon**
6T. **Florida State**
8. **Missouri**
9. **Mississippi**
10. **Ohio State**

September

FSU Says "Watch Out!": The first matchup of Top 10 teams ended with Florida State making a big leap into the national picture. The No. 8 Seminoles beat No. 5 LSU 45-24. FSU's **Jordan Travis** threw for 342 yards and had 4 TD passes. LSU gave up more points than any top-five team in its season opener . . . since 1968!

Coach Prime: NFL Hall of Famer **Deion "Prime Time" Sanders** took over as the coach at Colorado this season. The Buffaloes had won only one game in 2022, but "Coach Prime" turned things around. In the opener, Colorado upset No. 17 TCU 45-42. Its defense forced two turnovers, and QB **Shedeur Sanders** (the coach's son!) set a school record with 510 yards passing.

Duke Dominates: The ACC and the national playoff picture got an early scramble when unranked Duke beat No. 9 Clemson

Shedeur Sanders listens to coach (and dad!) Deion Sanders.

Trayanum lands in the end zone with a game-winning TD for Ohio State.

28-7. It was the Blue Devils' first win over a Top 10 team in 34 seasons!

Bama Bammed: No. 3 Alabama was surprised at home by No. 11 Texas. The Longhorns won 34-24, thanks to 3 TD passes by QB **Quinn Ewers**. It was the first home loss by Alabama in 21 games and its first regular-season nonconference loss in 57 games!

Need One More Player: No. 9 Notre Dame just needed to stop No. 6 Ohio State one more time to clinch a big win. But with one second left, **DeaMonte "Chip" Trayanum** banged in from the one-yard line and OSU won 17-14. After the play, Notre Dame coaches realized they had only 10 players on the field . . . and the score went right through where that player should have been! Oops!

Ewers shouts for joy after a win.

Gabriel (right) led Oklahoma to a big win over archrival Texas.

October

Defense? What Defense?: Defense took a day off when No. 20 Mississippi upset No. 13 LSU 55-49. Led by QB **Jaxson Dart**, Ole Miss rolled to 706 total yards. LSU was not far behind with 637! The Rebels ran for 317 yards, while Dart had 4 TD passes. The Tigers had to be disappointed that they scored 49 points but could not win.

Pac-12 Battle: No. 19 Oregon State traveled to No. 10 Utah and surprised the Utes with a 21-7 win. Though the Beavers were ranked higher, Utah was considered a favorite to meet USC for the conference title down the road. The OSU defense was the key, keeping Utah off the scoreboard until late in the fourth quarter.

Whew: Defending champ No. 1 Georgia escaped with a 27-20 win over unranked Auburn. The Bulldogs kept their national three-peat hopes alive with a late 40-yard TD pass from **Carson Beck** to **Brock Bowers** for the winning points.

Longhorns Lose: In 2024, the great Texas-Oklahoma rivalry moves to the SEC.

In 2023, the two teams left the Big 12 with another great memory as the Sooners scored late to upset the No. 3 Longhorns 34-30. Oklahoma QB **Dillon Gabriel**'s TD toss to **Nic Anderson** came with just 15 seconds left to disappoint a stadium full of Texas fans.

Streak Snapped:
No. 10 Notre Dame had won 30 straight regular-season ACC games until Louisville snapped it with a 33-20 win. The Louisville defense was great, sacking ND QB **Sam Hartman** five times and holding the Irish to just 44 rushing yards. The win moved 6–0 Louisville to No. 14 in the country!

That Was Too Close!:
No. 9 USC nearly lost to unranked Arizona but ended up on top 43-41 after three overtimes. QB **Caleb Williams**—the Heisman Trophy favorite—scored on a two-point play for the winning points. Still, Trojan fans were upset that their defense gave up so many points and worried about upcoming games!

What an Ending!:
With just 33 seconds left in the game, Miami only needed to kneel down to clinch a big win over Georgia Tech. But the Hurricanes ran the ball . . . and fumbled! In a miracle finish, Tech then moved the ball 74 yards, ending the game with a 44-yard TD catch by **Christian Leary** to win 23-20.

Trojans Fall:
USC Trojan fans were right to worry. USC lost to No. 21 Notre Dame 48-20. Williams threw 3 interceptions, while the ND defense and special teams scored in the game played at Notre Dame.

Top 10 Battle:
A pair of top Pac-12 teams met in a Top 10 showdown. No. 7 Washington scored late to defeat No. 8 Oregon 36-33. Huskies QB **Michael Penix Jr.** hit **Rome Odunze** with a TD pass with less than two minutes left for the clinching score in a fantastic, back-and-forth game.

Into the Lake!:
That's where Kansas fans dumped the goalposts after their team shocked No. 6 Oklahoma 38-33. It was the first time in 19 games that Kansas had won the Midwest matchup. **Devin Neal** scored the winning TD with less than a minute left. When the game ended, fans stormed the field and nabbed the goalposts in celebration!

Stunning Comeback:
Stanford was behind Colorado 29-0 at halftime. A lot of fans left . . . but they missed the biggest comeback in school history! Stanford rallied to tie the score at 36-36. The teams needed two overtimes to decide a winner, with Stanford K **Joshua Karty**'s 31-yard field goal as the winning points: Stanford 46-43. Stanford WR **Elic Ayomanor** set a school record with 294 receiving yards, including a miracle TD catch off a defender's helmet!

Ayomanor caught ball and helmet!

November

Super D: Iowa had a remarkable defense all sesaon long. The Hawkeyes' amazing D allowed 10 or fewer points in six games. In November, the team gave up only 30 total points as they won four straight games. But the offense struggled. Iowa won 10 games but scored only 20 offensive TDs and zero points in their final two games.

Bye-Bye, Bedlam: Oklahoma and Oklahoma State have been playing each other every season since 1910. But with OU moving to a new conference in 2024, the series ended . . . but not the way OU wanted. Oklahoma State shocked the No. 10 Sooners 27-24. **Ollie Gordon II** had a pair of rushing TDs. OSU fans were so thrilled that they tore down the goalposts!

Nix lit up the scoreboard against ASU.

Mighty Michigan: Who needs passing? The No. 2 Wolverines dominated No. 9 Penn State to set themselves up as a real national title contender. Michigan ran the ball for 32 straight plays starting late in the first half, ending in a **Blake Corum** TD run. Keeping the ball away from the Nittany Lions led to a 24-15 win. The Michigan D had allowed only 75 total points in the team's 10 straight wins. (A week later, Michigan beat Maryland for the school's 1,000th victory all-time, the most ever.)

Huskies Escape: No. 5 Washington survived playing one of its worst games— and a wild Northwest rainstorm—to beat Oregon State 22-20. The Huskies led in the fourth quarter, but the Beavers bit back, closing to within two points before Washington could wrap up the game.

Good News, Bad News: No. 4 Florida State continued its awesome season, pounding North Alabama 58-13. However, star QB **Jordan Travis** hurt his leg and was out for the rest of the game . . . and the season. Would the Seminoles be able to bounce back and stay in the Playoff picture?

Nix Quacks: Oregon moved to 10–1 with an eye on the College Football Playoff with a 49-13 win over Arizona State. Heisman Trophy candidate QB **Bo Nix** had 6 TD passes for the Ducks, along with 404 passing yards.

Big Ten Battle: For the third year in a row, No. 3 Michigan came out on top in their annual rivalry game with No. 2 Ohio State.

Milroe led Alabama around a fierce Auburn defense to avoid an upset.

Led by Corum's 2 TDs, the Wolverines gave the Buckeyes their first loss 30-24. Michigan was one win away from another trip to the College Football Playoff.

Alabama Miracle: No. 8 Alabama escaped a huge upset in its own rivalry game, the Iron Bowl with Auburn. **Jalen Milroe** threw a TD pass on fourth-and-goal from the 31-yard line with just 32 seconds left. **Isaiah Bond** caught it to give Bama a shocking 27-24 win. It was one of the biggest final-play wins of the season in college football.

Washington–WSU: The Apple Cup is the game between Washington and Washington State. With UW moving to the Big Ten in 2024, this year's might have been the last. The game came down to a final play. **Grady Gross** kicked a 42-yard field goal to give the No. 4 Huskies a 24-21 win over a gutsy Cougars team. In the locker room after the game, Gross was awarded a full football scholarship in thanks for his timely kick.

Gross won the game . . . and a scholarship.

Conference Championships

Corum dives for yardage in a Big Ten win.

RB **Blake Corum** pounded in for two TDs, while the Wolverines' D allowed the Hawkeyes only 155 total yards in a rout that left Michigan at No. 1 in the country.

BIG 12 Texas 49 / Oklahoma State 21

Longhorns QB **Quinn Ewers** threw 4 TD passes as Texas wrapped up a 12–1 season by winning the conference for the first time in 14 seasons. It was also their last game in the conference, as they move to the SEC in 2024.

SEC Alabama 27 / Georgia 24

The Crimson Tide leaped into the Playoff by ending two-time defending champ Georgia's 29-game winning streak. Bama QB **Jalen Milroe** had a great game, throwing 2 TD passes and leading the offense to 306 total yards. The loss knocked Georgia out of the Playoff.

PAC-12 Washington 34 / Oregon 31

The Ducks lost only twice in 2023, both times to the Huskies and both times by only three points. Washington's win here sent them into the College Football Playoff. Oregon QB **Bo Nix** had 3 TD passes, but they were not enough in the end.

ACC Florida State 16 / Louisville 6

The Seminoles wrapped up a perfect 13–0 season with their first conference title since 2014. But they had to use third-string QB **Brock Glenn** to do it, because of injuries to other players. Without star QB **Jordan Travis**, FSU was forced out of the Playoff in a very controversial decision.

BIG TEN Michigan 26 / Iowa 0

Iowa's great defense finally met an offense it could not stop. Michigan

Glenn led FSU to an ACC title.

Key Bowl Games

Bowl season began December 16 with a very long schedule of 41 bowl games! Here are a few highlights from the 2023 bowls.

FABULOUS FILL-IN: USC was led all season by 2022 Heisman winner **Caleb Williams**. But he headed to the NFL Draft and did not play in the team's Holiday Bowl game. **Miller Moss** stepped in and all he did was throw 6 TD passes in his first college start! The Trojans stomped Louisville 42-28.

FOOD BOWLS: Two bowl games had food-company sponsors and added splashes of oddness to their games. West Virginia coach **Neal Brown** was covered with actual mayonnaise after his team beat North Carolina 30-10 in the Duke's Mayo Bowl. After Kansas beat NC State 28-19 in the Pop-Tarts Bowl, the Pop-Tarts mascot actually went into a toaster . . . and slid out as a pastry enjoyed by the winning team.

BIG COMEBACK: Most bowl games are not that thrilling, with both teams wrapping up their seasons with little to play for. Don't tell that to the No. 14 Arizona Wildcats. They forced six turnovers on the way to a 38-24 win over No. 6 Oklahoma. Arizona trailed 24-13 but then scored the final 25 points of the game to win the Alamo Bowl.

BULLDOGS BITE BIG: The No. 6 Georgia Bulldogs set a record by beating No. 5 Florida State 63-3 in the Orange Bowl. The 60-point difference was the biggest in college bowl game history! Undefeated FSU was starting its third-string QB after being left out of the College Football Playoff.

Yes, that is mayo being dumped on Brown.

College Football Semifinals

McCarthy "rose" to the occasion.

Michigan 27, Alabama 20 (OT)

The Rose Bowl was the host of the first of two thrilling semifinals, both of which came down to the final play. The Wolverines finally won a Playoff semifinal after losing in 2021 and 2022. They needed a big TD run from RB **Blake Corum** in overtime to beat the Crimson Tide. Michigan QB **J.J. McCarthy** had 3 TD passes, including a four-yarder to **Roman Wilson** to tie the score with less than two minutes left. In OT, Michigan got the ball first and Corum set a new all-time Michigan rushing TD mark on a 17-yard run. Alabama then got the ball and advanced to the Michigan three-yard line. A low snap slowed the action, and Bama QB **Jalen Milroe** was stopped by the Michigan line.

Washington 37, Texas 31

In the Sugar Bowl, the Longhorns made things exciting, coming back to have a chance at victory on the final play, but Washington stopped them. The Huskies thought they had the game in hand when they were up 34-21. QB **Michael Penix Jr.** was lights-out on his way to 430 passing yards and 2 TDs. But Texas got a TD pass from **Quinn Ewers** to pull within six points. Each team added a field goal. Then Texas got one more shot late in the game. They reached the Washington 13-yard line but could not reach the end zone in four plays, sending the Huskies to the championship game—the first for the Pac-12 since 2014.

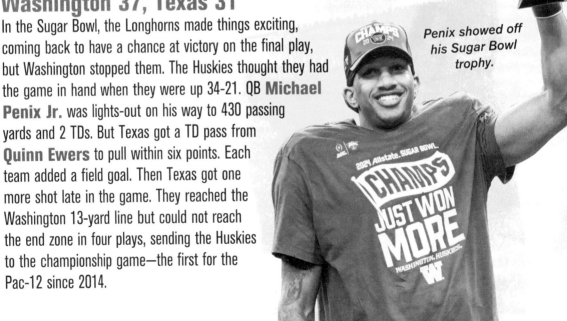

Penix showed off his Sugar Bowl trophy.

National Championship Game

MICHIGAN 34, WASHINGTON 13

The Wolverines' long wait was over. Even though they are one of the winningest and most famous college teams, Michigan had not been a solo national champ since 1948. (They shared a national title in 1997.) By stomping Washington, Michigan finally brought the national title back home, piling up 303 rushing yards in a dominant win. RB **Donovan Edwards** was the first spark. The speedy back ran 41 and 46 yards for TDs in the first quarter! **Blake Corum** added a 59-yard run that led to a second-quarter field goal.

Meanwhile, the Michigan D kept Huskies star QB **Michael Penix Jr.** quiet. Pressure made him miss key throws, but he did throw a late TD to make the halftime score closer at 17-10.

Michigan began the second half by picking off a pass by Penix. Even with Michigan controlling both sides of the line, the score was only 20-13 as the fourth quarter began. A long Michigan drive ended with a Corum TD run. Another interception by Michigan and a second Corum TD sealed the big win. For his two scores and 134 rushing yards, Corum was named offensive MVP. **Will Johnson** was the defensive MVP for his second-half interception and great work stopping the run.

Michigan finished as the sixth team ever with a perfect 15–0. It was a sweet W for the Wolverines, who had lost in the previous two Playoffs. The school fight song was finally really true: "Hail to the Victors!"

Corum kept up his TD-scoring ways.

Division I Awards

HEISMAN TROPHY
AP PLAYER OF THE YEAR
DAVEY O'BRIEN AWARD
UNITAS GOLDEN ARM AWARD
WALTER CAMP AWARD
Jayden Daniels, QB, LSU ▶

BILETNIKOFF AWARD
Marvin Harrison Jr., WR,
Ohio State

DOAK WALKER AWARD
Ollie Gordon II, RB, Ohio State

NAGURSKI AWARD
Xavier Watts, S, Notre Dame

BUTKUS AWARD
Payton Wilson, LB,
North Carolina State

LOMBARDI AWARD
Laiatu Latu, DE, UCLA

LOU GROZA AWARD
Graham Nicholson, K,
Miami of Ohio

Located in Arkansas, Harding University captured the Division II national title.

Other NCAA Champs

FCS

South Dakota State 23, Montana 3

The Jackrabbits won their second straight title. QB **Mark Gronowski** ran for 1 TD and threw a TD pass before hoisting the trophy again.

Division II

Harding 38, Colorado School of Mines 7

Harding won the school's first-ever national championship, led by a clock-eating running attack.

Division III

Cortland 38, North Central 37

North Central, from Illinois, tried to win its second straight title by going for two after its final score. But Cortland, from New York, held on and won its first national title.

NAIA

Keiser 31, Northwestern 21

Florida's Keiser knocked off Iowa's Northwestern to become yet another first-time national champ.

WNBA/NBA

BACK-TO-BACK!

Sydney Colson is thrilled to have helped the Las Vegas Aces earn their second-straight WNBA championship with a four-game win over the New York Liberty. The Aces were led once again by superstar A'ja Wilson. Read on for more about the awesome 2023 WNBA season.

A NEW ALL-TIME CHAMP!
Jayson Tatum lets the world know how psyched he is as his Boston Celtics win their NBA-record 18th championship. Boston beat the Dallas Mavericks in five games to win the 2023–24 title. The series capped off a terrific NBA season that had new stars rising all over the league! Read on to find out more!

In 2023, Stewart (right) changed teams but kept up her MVP-level performance.

WNBA 2023

Before the 2023 season, two WNBA teams piled up a stack of stars. All-around hero **Breanna Stewart** and passing wizard **Courtney Vandersloot** joined the New York Liberty. There they joined shooting star **Sabrina Ionescu** to form a kind of superteam. Meanwhile, the Las Vegas Aces, the defending champs, also got better with the addition of **Candace Parker**. Would

these two teams meet for the title? To find out, everyone had to play the 2023 season first!

Attention on opening day turned to Los Angeles, where **Brittney Griner** of the Phoenix Mercury returned to play the Los Angeles Sparks after missing the 2022 season. Griner had been detained and imprisoned in Russia for about 10 months before she was finally freed. Griner scored the first bucket of the game in her home return, as fans filled the air with cheers of welcome!

As the season started, Vegas had a historic beginning. They won their first 10 games in a row, setting a team record. The Liberty lost a couple of games early, but once they got used to one another, the superteam started to win big. By the middle of the season, they were 16–1 and finished with 32 wins. But by the end of the season, the Aces did even better, setting a new single-season WNBA mark of 34 wins.

The Connecticut Sun lost the 2022 WNBA Finals but got off to a hot start in 2023 to try to correct that. Led by **Brionna Jones**, they opened up 9–3 and wound up third in the league at 27–13.

The season was packed with players setting records. Stewart became the first player in WNBA history to reach 200 points, 100 rebounds, and 40 assists in her team's first 10 games. In September, she broke the single-season scoring record with 861 points. But when the dust settled after the regular season, **Jewell Loyd** had topped Stewart to set a new all-time best with 939. **Alyssa Thomas** set a single-season assist record with 316 dimes.

On August 6, the great **Diana Taurasi** of the Phoenix Mercury added to her long list of records. She became the first WNBA player to score over 10,000 points in a career. Later that month, **A'ja Wilson** of Las Vegas tied a league record with 53 points in a game, when her team beat Atlanta 112-100.

Once the playoffs started, the records didn't matter—it all came down to winning, no matter what.

Commissioner's Cup

The WNBA runs an in-season tournament among all its teams called the Commissioner's Cup. The games do not count in the regular-season standings. The Liberty earned the 2023 Cup by knocking off the Aces 82-63. Would Las Vegas get revenge in the WNBA Finals?

WNBA 2023 Awards

MOST VALUABLE PLAYER
Breanna Stewart, Liberty

DEFENSIVE PLAYER OF THE YEAR
A'ja Wilson, Aces

ROOKIE OF THE YEAR
Aliyah Boston, Fever

MOST IMPROVED PLAYER
Satou Sabally, Wings

SIXTH PLAYER OF THE YEAR
Alysha Clark, Aces

WNBA STATS LEADERS

24.7 POINTS PER GAME
Jewell Loyd, Storm

9.9 REBOUNDS PER GAME
Alyssa Thomas, Sun

8.1 ASSISTS PER GAME
Courtney Vandersloot, Liberty

128 THREE-POINTERS
Sabrina Ionescu, Liberty

Boston was so good in 2023, even her hair played well!

Jones (left) led the Liberty into the WNBA Finals with gritty play like this.

2023 WNBA Playoffs

FIRST ROUND

Las Vegas easily won its first-round playoff series over the Chicago Sky, while No. 2 seed New York swept the Washington Mystics. The Dallas Wings beat the Atlanta Dream, while the Connecticut Sky needed three games to advance over the Minnesota Lynx.

SEMIFINALS

Aces 3, Wings 0

Superstar **A'ja Wilson** led the way as usual, scoring 34 points in a Game 1 win. That was just the start of a three-game Aces sweep that sent the defending champs back to the WNBA Finals. Dallas made the third game tight, but the Aces scored the game's final five baskets to win 64-61.

Liberty 3, Sun 1

The Sun surprised the favored Liberty to win Game 1. The Connecticut D held the Liberty to 63 points, its lowest score of the season. But New York rallied behind its roster of stars to win the series and return to the Finals for the first time since 2002. With MVP **Breanna Stewart** pouring in points, the Liberty got big help in the clinching Game 4 from another former MVP, **Jonquel Jones**, who had 25 points in an 87-84 win.

Aces 3, Liberty 1
WNBA Finals

Plum (left) joined teammate Gray in helping lead the Aces to a Game 1 win.

GAME 1 Aces 99, Liberty 82

Fans had been waiting for this battle between the WNBA's two star-studded superteams since the season's opening tip-off. The Aces' **Chelsea Gray** picked the right day to have her best game of the year. She put in 26 points—teammate **Kelsey Plum** matched her—and Las Vegas won Game 1. Oh, and it was also Gray's 31st birthday . . . a great way to celebrate!

GAME 2 Aces 104, Liberty 76

Talk about a fast start! Las Vegas was ahead 21-4 before the Liberty even took off their warmup clothes! The Aces never looked back, led by **A'ja Wilson**'s 26 points and 15 rebounds. It was her second double-double of the playoffs. Liberty star **Breanna Stewart** had only 14 points.

GAME 3 Liberty 87, Aces 73

When you're in big trouble, you need superheroes. Good thing the Liberty have two: former MVPs **Jonquel Jones** and Stewart. In a game they had to win, Jones went for 27 and B-Stew had a double-double to keep the Liberty alive. Defense was also key. Plum put in 29 for the Aces, but otherwise, the Liberty kept the big Las Vegas stars quiet.

GAME 4 Aces 70, Liberty 69

With Gray out with an injury, could the Liberty even the series? They came close, but in the end the Aces won their second-straight WNBA championship. Wilson was the Finals MVP after a 24-point double-double in the clinching game. The Liberty led most of the way, but Vegas roared back. New York's **Courtney Vandersloot** had a shot at the buzzer for the win but missed. The Aces celebrated the first repeat WNBA championship in 21 seasons.

A'ja Wilson

NBA 2023-24

On one side of the country, an NBA team ran away with its conference. On the other, several teams battled until the final Sunday to see who ended up on top. And that was just the regular season! The NBA in 2023–24 was packed with high scoring, some familiar superstars, and a new crop of young players who brought lots of excitement.

For the first half of the season, the big story was high scoring. There was a flurry of games that saw big stars put up big points. Dallas's **Luka Dončić** led the way with 73 points in a January game (see more of Dončić's scoring success on page 93). That was tied for the fourth-most in a game in NBA history! Two-time scoring champ **Joel Embiid** nearly matched him with 70. Earlier in the season, the magical two-time MVP **Giannis Antetokounmpo** put up 64. **Karl-Anthony Towns** and **Devin Booker** each scored 62 points in a game.

As for those best teams in each conference, in the East, it was the Boston Celtics—by far. They won 64 games, their most since 2008, and won the conference by 14 games. Slipping into second were the surprising New York

Knicks. Point guard **Jalen Brunson** emerged as a scoring force, driving New York to the No. 2 seed. The Milwaukee Bucks, after a slow start and a pep talk from Antetokounmpo, ended up third. A big reason was point guard **Damian "Dame Time" Lillard**, who had joined the team from Portland. His leadership worked well with Antetokounmpo's magic to lead the Bucks to 49 wins.

In the West, several teams took a big leap. The Minnesota Timberwolves had the league's best record through 20 games (one-quarter of the season) and were best in the West in the first half. The Oklahoma City Thunder were not far behind, thanks to the play of C **Chet Holmgren** and G **Shai Gilgeous-Alexander**, who moved into the top ranks of all-around NBA players this season. And the Denver Nuggets will always be great as long as megastar **Nikola Jokić** is around. The big man continued to light up the scoreboard (and win his third MVP!) as well as pass out perfect dimes. The Thunder ended up with the No. 1 seed. Not bad for a team

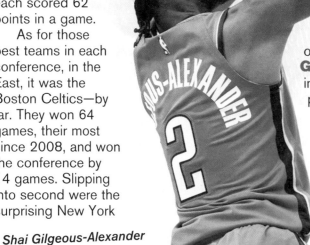

Shai Gilgeous-Alexander

that didn't even make the playoffs in 2022–23.

Joining them in the playoffs was a host of other great teams led by veterans and rising stars. The Los Angeles Lakers, of course, had "The King," **LeBron James**, who put the team on his back again and led them to the postseason. The Indiana Pacers had the season's surprise star, **Tyrese Haliburton**. He made his second All-Star team and led the league in assists for the first time.

Two teams, however, had seasons to forget. The Detroit Pistons had an epic losing streak. Detroit lost 28 games in a row, setting

"Wemby" shows off his shot-blocking form.

a new NBA all-time single-season record that no team wants to own. Meanwhile, the San Antonio Spurs lost 18 games in a row, a team record. However, they did feature the outstanding rookie **Victor Wembanyama**, a 7-foot-4 shot-blocking star who also poured in points. An easy choice for the Rookie of the Year, he was the second first-year player to lead the league in blocks.

While those two teams watched—along with NBA fans around the world—the NBA playoffs and Finals were as awesome and exciting as always.

Read on!

2023–24 FINAL NBA STANDINGS

EASTERN CONFERENCE

ATLANTIC DIVISION		CENTRAL DIVISION		SOUTHEAST DIVISION	
Celtics	64–18	Bucks	49–33	Magic	47–35
Knicks	50–32	Cavaliers	48–34	Heat	46–36
76ers	47–35	Pacers	47–35	Hawks	36–46
Nets	32–50	Bulls	39–43	Hornets	21–61
Raptors	25–57	Pistons	14–68	Wizards	15–67

WESTERN CONFERENCE

NORTHWEST DIVISION		SOUTHWEST DIVISION		PACIFIC DIVISION	
Thunder	57–25	Mavericks	50–32	Clippers	51–31
Nuggets	57–25	Pelicans	49–33	Suns	49–33
Timberwolves	56–26	Rockets	41–41	Lakers	47–35
Jazz	31–51	Grizzlies	27–55	Kings	46–36
Trail Blazers	21–61	Spurs	22–60	Warriors	46–36

In the Paint

Young was unstoppable!

Hot Streak: Trae Young of the

Atlanta Hawks did something that has not been done for 59 seasons! The multitalented guard ran off seven straight games with at least 30 points and 10 assists. Only the great **Oscar Robertson** had a streak that long, which he achieved way back in 1964–65.

Cold Streak: Detroit tied an

unfortunate NBA record by losing 28 games in a row. They almost snapped the streak against the No. 1 Celtics, but finally won 129-127 over the Toronto Raptors. **Cade Cunningham** led the way with 30 points in the (whew!) win.

Big Bucket by Big Man:

Everybody knows **Nikola Jokić** of the Nuggets is one of the NBA's best. After all, he has three NBA MVP trophies and an NBA title. But who knew he could hit from nearly half-court? That's what he did on January 4 at the buzzer to beat Golden State 130-127.

Wonderful Wemby:

Super tall with point-guard ball skills and a good outside shot, **Victor Wembanyama** is one of a kind. The French rookie for the Spurs put on a show around the country. He had his first triple-double just 32 games into the season, then had another that included 10 blocks! He was the first rookie ever with 1,500 points, 250 assists, and 250 blocks. His 3.6 blocks per game was the most in the league, too.

GOAT Battle: LeBron James

is the NBA's all-time scoring leader. **Stephen Curry** is the best ever at three-point shooting. Their teams have had lots of big matchups, but in January, the stars had their first regular-season overtime game. In fact, they had so much fun, they made it *double* OT. In the end, it

Dončić had a record-setting streak.

was a boring old free throw by James that gave his Lakers a 145-144 win over Curry's Warriors.

Half-court Heave:
With Super Bowl champs **Patrick Mahomes** and **Travis Kelce** in the seats, Cleveland's **Max Strus** had a night to remember. In a game against Dallas, Strus made seven three-pointers. The last of those was a 59-foot buzzer-beater that won the game 121-119.

Luka Does Even Better:
Along with scoring 73 points in one game, **Luka Dončić** grabbed his own place in the NBA record book. On March 9, he scored 39 points while grabbing 10 rebounds and passing out 10 assists in a Mavericks win over the Pistons. That gave him six straight games with a triple-double that included at least 30 points— a new NBA all-time best streak!

IN-SEASON TOURNAMENT

For the first time, the NBA played a tournament during its regular season. Many European soccer leagues do this, and the NBA was trying to jazz up early-season games. Each team played three Cup games as part of its regular schedule. The top four teams played in a knockout tournament in Las Vegas. In the championship game, the ageless wonder **LeBron James** (right) led the Lakers to victory. Teammate **Anthony Davis** had a monster game with 41 points and 20 rebounds, plus 4 blocks. The IST turned out to be a big hit with players and fans.

NBA Playoffs

Win or go home! Here are some playoff highlights from an exciting month of games:

➤ **Jalen Brunson** of the Knicks scored at least 40 points and had 5 assists in four straight playoff games, an NBA first.

Brunson (11) dominated the Philadelphia 76ers in the first round of the playoffs.

➤ To beat the Magic in Game 7 of the first roun the Cavaliers came back from 18 points down It was the largest Game 7 comeback since 1997!

➤ Indiana won a series for the first time since 2014. The Pacers' **T.J. McConnell** set a playoff career high with 20 points as his tean upset the Bucks in six games.

➤ Missing stars: **LeBron James**, **Stephen Curry**, and **Kevin Durant** all lost in the firs round. It was the first time at least one of then was not in the second round since 2005!

➤ Dallas upset No. 1 seed Oklahoma City in an exciting six-game series.

➤ Down 3–2 in games to the Nuggets, the Timberwolves blew up. Their 115-70 win was the biggest point spread ever by a team beating a defending champion. Then in Game they trailed by 20 points in the second half . . and WON 98-90. Thrilling series!

➤ In beating the Knicks 130-109 in the Eastern Conference semifinals Game 7, the Pacers set an NBA playoff record by shooting 67.1 percent.

Eastern Conference Final
CELTICS 4, PACERS 0

A **Jaylen Brown** three-pointer near the buzzer sent Game 1 into overtime. The Celtics ended up winning 133-128. Brown was the hero of Game 2 as well, pouring in a game-high 40 points as the Celtics won by 16 points. In Game 3, the Pacers led for most of the night, piling up an 18-point lead at one point. But the Celtics came back strong, led by **Jayson Tatum**'s 36 points. The key moment was a three-point play by **Jrue Holiday** with less than a minute left. He added two free throws to clinch a 114-111 win. A three-pointer by **Derrick White** was the difference in Boston's Game 4 win. The sweep sent the Celtics to their second NBA Finals in three seasons.

Western Conference Final
MAVERICKS 4, TIMBERWOLVES 1

Kyrie Irving had a 24-point first half and **Luka Dončić** had a 15-point fourth quarter. The Mavericks' star pair combined to lead Dallas to a 108-105 Game 1 upset over Minnesota. Dončić showed off his clutch shooting by nailing a three-point shot with just three seconds left in Game 2, and Dallas won 109-108. The Mavs' power duo had 33 points each in Game 3, and Dallas won by nine. Minnesota avoided a sweep thanks to big Game 4 scoring from **Karl-Anthony Towns** and **Anthony Edwards**. Dallas won Game 5 124-103 to clinch the series, led by 36 points each from the dynamic duo of Dončić and Irving.

Irving (right) helped lead the Mavericks back to their first NBA Finals since 2011.

NBA Finals

Finals MVP Brown rose above Dallas!

GAME 1
BOSTON 107, DALLAS 89

A 17-point first-quarter lead got Boston off to a strong start on its homecourt. Behind a strong game by **Jaylen Brown**, the Celtics stretched the lead to 29 in the first half before cruising to a key Game 1 win. Boston fans loved seeing big man **Kristaps Porzingis** return after a month-long injury layoff. He poured in 20 points and helped guard Dallas superstar **Luka Dončić** (who still scored 30 points). Boston had six players reach double figures, showing the all-around depth that helped them earn the NBA's top record in 2023–24.

GAME 2
BOSTON 105, DALLAS 98

That depth showed again in Boston's Game 2 win. This time it was guard **Jrue Holiday** leading the way, scoring a team-high 26 points. The team also showed off strong defense, with **Derrick White** blocking a key late Dallas shot to help keep Boston on top. Dončić still managed a triple-double, the first such Finals game in Dallas history, but it was not enough. Celtics star **Jayson Tatum** didn't score as much as usual, but he had 12 assists and 9 rebounds!

GAME 3
BOSTON 106, DALLAS 99

On their home court, the Mavs almost made a miraculous comeback. They trailed the Celtics by as much as 21 points in the second half. A fourth-quarter run, led as usual by Dončić, brought them within three.

Dončić (right) led all scorers with 146 total points.

led the way again for Dallas with 29 points as the Mavericks prevented a Celtics sweep.

GAME 5
BOSTON 106, DALLAS 88

The Celtics set a new NBA record with their 18th championship, breaking a tie with the Lakers. Tatum had 31 points and 11 assists, the first 30 and 10 NBA Finals game in the long history of the Celtics. He and Brown had played 107 playoff games together, the most ever by two players without a title. Teammate **Al Horford** had played 186 playoff games without a title, among the most ever. Another highlight was a halftime-buzzer-beating half-court three-pointer by **Payton Pritchard** that had Celtics fans screaming for joy! Brown was named the Bill Russell NBA Finals MVP, an award named for a Celtics great who was a part of 11 of the team's 18 titles. In the end, the team with the season's best record came through with the best Finals performance.

But Dončić fouled out with just over four minutes left. Dallas got within one point, but White hit a key three-pointer, while the Dallas treys all missed. The Celtics made their late free throws and held on for a big win.

GAME 4
DALLAS 122, BOSTON 84

Did the Celtics forget when this game started? From almost the first moments, they did not look like the team that had won three straight. Dallas dominated at both ends of the court. At one point they led by 48 points! It ended up being the biggest NBA Finals loss ever for Boston, and the third-biggest in NBA history! Dončić

Tatum finally got to lift the NBA championship trophy!

2023–24 Stat Leaders

(per-game averages, except for three-pointer total)

33.9 POINTS
Luka Dončić
MAVERICKS

13.7 REBOUNDS
Domantas Sabonis
KINGS

10.9 ASSISTS
Tyrese Haliburton
PACERS

3.6 BLOCKS
Victor Wembanyama
SPURS

2.0 STEALS
De'Aaron Fox
KINGS

357 THREE-POINTERS
Stephen Curry ▶▶▶
WARRIORS

2024 NBA Awards

MOST VALUABLE PLAYER
NIKOLA JOKIĆ ▶▶▶
NUGGETS

DEFENSIVE PLAYER OF THE YEAR
RUDY GOBERT
TIMBERWOLVES

ROOKIE OF THE YEAR
VICTOR WEMBANYAMA
SPURS

SIXTH MAN OF THE YEAR
NAZ REID
TIMBERWOLVES

MOST IMPROVED PLAYER
TYRESE MAXEY
76ERS

COACH OF THE YEAR
MARK DAIGNEAULT
THUNDER

COLLEGE BASKETBALL

BACK-TO-BACK!
Connecticut (including Stephon Castle, above) won its second men's title in a row, the first team to do that since 2007. They swarmed through a tough NCAA tourney, winning all their games by double digits. The Huskies capped off their title run with a 75-60 win over National Player of the Year Zach Edey and Purdue. Can they go for three in 2025?

CHAMPS . . . AGAIN!
South Carolina completed a perfect season by beating Iowa in the national championship. The Gamecocks (led by Kamilla Cardoso, above) were 38–0 and knocked off Caitlin Clark and Iowa 87-75. It was SC's second win in three seasons and third overall. The game capped off one of the best seasons—okay, let's say it . . . THE BEST SEASON ever for women's college sports. What will 2025 look like?

College Hoops

Caitlin
Clark

In 2023–24, the biggest story in college basketball—maybe in all of sports—was a woman. The amazing **Caitlin Clark**, with help from her Iowa Hawkeyes teammates, blew up the sport with record-shattering shooting and serious swag. Clark brought more viewers to the sport than ever before, which included the most-watched NCAA game of the year with 24 million viewers. That was 10 million more than the men's final, the first time the women have been number one! And the women's national championship game had 10 million more people watching in 2024 than they had in 2023. Wow! In an earlier round, Clark starred in another big matchup, the rematch of the year–Iowa vs. LSU. That game had 12.3 million viewers. Safe to say, the sports world will not forget the collegiate career of Caitlin Clark. America was thrilled as she chased down and beat the all-time career scoring records for women and then for men. Along the way, she set single-season records for points (1,234) and three-pointers (201), too!

Clark, who stands at an even six feet tall, was not the only record setter this year. On the men's side, a player who stood 16 inches taller achieved something that had not been done in decades! Purdue's **Zach Edey** was the face of the men's game all the way through March. No one else had won back-to-back National Player of the Year awards since **Ralph Sampson** in 1983.

As usual, the college season included its fair share of upsets. Let's face it, if not for those pesky Cinderellas, the sport just wouldn't be as fun. But by the end of the year, however, a pair of powerhouse schools faced off in both the men's and women's national championship games. Cinderellas don't always get a happy ending!

Edey (right) was a force on offense and defense for the Boilermakers.

For some teams, the chase for glory in March was about creating a dynasty (hello, Huskies and Gamecocks!). For others, it was about doing something that had never been done in their school's history (hello, North Carolina State!). As the confetti finally fell on March Madness, the champions emerged. But from start to finish, the 2023–24 season of college basketball was must-see TV to the final buzzer.

FINAL MEN'S AP TOP 10

1. Connecticut
2. Purdue
3. Alabama
4. Houston
5. Tennessee
6. Illinois
7. North Carolina
8. Iowa State
9. Duke
10. NC State

FINAL WOMEN'S TOP 10

1. South Carolina
2. Iowa
3. Connecticut
4. NC State
5. USC
6. LSU
7. Texas
8. Oregon State
9. Stanford
10. UCLA

Men's Notes

Connecticut was the first of Seton Hall's upset victims.

A Pirate's Life: The Seton Hall Pirates served as a bit of a spoiler for ranked teams in the Big East. The first upset was the most exciting for the Pirates—a convincing 75-60 win against No. 5 UConn. After handing it to the defending champs, the Pirates knocked off No. 23 Providence soon after. Then Seton Hall did it again just after New Year's against No. 7 Marquette. The Pirates won a tight contest 78-75 to continue their momentum. The second time around, all three of those teams got the better of the Pirates, but those three upsets were a lot of fun!

THIS Is Sparta?: In the preseason AP Top 25 poll, the Michigan State Spartans were ranked fourth. The high hopes did not last long for the Spartans. Unranked James Madison defeated them in the Spartans' own gym on opening night! To be fair, James Madison did finish the year 32-4, but who knew that at the time? Michigan State took a while to get up and running, losing five of their first nine contests before righting the ship. The Spartans did qualify for the NCAA tournament, but for a season with Final Four hopes, a 20–15 record did not sit well in East Lansing.

Every Winning Streak Starts After a Loss:

Have you heard that saying before? Well, for Connecticut, after that loss to Seton Hall just before Christmas, the Huskies didn't lose again until after Valentine's Day. After dropping their Big East opener, UConn rattled off 14 straight wins. The last was a big 81-53 over No. 4 Marquette. The 28-point difference between two teams was the biggest ever between top-five ranked teams. With that, UConn took a clear hold of the No. 1 spot in the nation, a spot they held on to until April.

Man of the Year: Purdue's seven-foot-four, 300-pound superstar Zach Edey put the Boilermakers on his back this season. Edey averaged over 25 points per game and was named Big Ten Player of the Year (again). Edey's finest night came on February 25 at Michigan. The big man scored 35 points in an 84-76 win. At year's end, Edey won the John R. Wooden Award. For the second straight year, he got all the first-place votes, too. He added a sweep of the other five major national awards as well.

Stung by Yellow Jackets:
Georgia Tech did not have a great season. They ended with a 14–18 record, 12th place in the ACC. But they can look back with pride on doing something very rare. They managed to beat both Duke and North Carolina in the same season, the top two finishers in the ACC.

Long Beach's Jason Hart Jr. celebrates!

A pair of Yellow Jackets buzzing after a win.

Last Chance Long Beach: This could qualify as a postseason highlight, but we're putting it here because it started in the regular season. Long Beach State ended their Big West regular season by losing five games in a row. The school announced that head coach Dan Monson would be fired when the conference tournament was over. The fun part? Long Beach then rallied behind Monson and ended up *winning* the Big West Tournament. That gave the team their first trip to the NCAA tournament in 12 years. The awkward part? The Cinderella season—and Monson's job at LBSU—ended with a first-round loss to Arizona. But it was a great and memorable run.

Women's Notes

South Carolina said "bonjour!" to Paris!

Everyone Watches:
In 2024, the saying was everywhere—"Everyone Watches Women's Sports." The TV viewer numbers back that up, but who would have thought that "everyone" included . . . the French? On November 6, 2023, South Carolina walloped Notre Dame 100-71 in the NCAA's first women's game to ever take place in Paris.

A Rocky (Mountain) Start:
On Thursday, November 9, the LSU Tigers raised their championship banner and received their rings in their home opener. They had to find something to cheer about, after all. LSU had lost their season opener to Colorado just three days prior. After beginning their historic 2022–23 season with 23 wins in a row, the preseason No. 1 team in the nation was 0–1 right out of the gate. (Don't worry, they came back to make the national quarterfinals.)

She Stands Alone:
On January 21 against Oregon State, Stanford head coach Tara VanDerveer made history by winning her 1,203rd game. She had topped Pat Summitt's women's record in 2020. This time, VanDerveer passed Mike Krzyzewski to give her the most wins in NCAA basketball history. At year's end, the legendary coach announced her retirement, finishing with 1,216 wins, including a 2021 national championship at Stanford.

Battle of Champs:
In a battle of the two most recent national champions, South Carolina continued their perfect season with a 76-70 win over LSU. The big play was thanks to a Bree Hall go-ahead three-pointer in the final minutes. Props to LSU, though: the six-point margin was the closest any team got to beating South Carolina in the regular season.

UConn was thrilled by Bueckers' return.

Return of the Queen: UConn's **Paige Bueckers** went nearly 600 days in between games due to injuries. When she finally got back on the court, she was named the Big East Player of the Year, just as she was as a freshman back in 2021. In conference play, the junior averaged 22 points per game. The Huskies were 18–0 in the conference and beat Georgetown 78-42 in the conference title game. After her long time out, Bueckers was the Big East Tournament Most Outstanding Player and Player of the Year.

The Greatest of All Time?

Caitlin Clark was the biggest story in basketball this year. She got that way by piling up historic numbers.

- ▶ February 15: Clark scored 49 points to break Kelsey Plum's NCAA women's basketball all-time scoring record.

- ▶ March 3: Clark added 35 more points to go past LSU's Pete Maravich, who had held the NCAA all-time record of 3,667 points. She ended with 3,951.

- ▶ Her 548 career three-pointers are a new record, beating Taylor Robertson, who set the mark only the previous season.

- ▶ For 2023–24, Clark poured in 1,234 points, including 201 three-pointers, both new NCAA single-season records.

- ▶ Her 346 assists led the NCAA as well, showing off her all-around game.

She capped off an incredible year by being the first overall pick in the WNBA Draft, chosen by the Indiana Fever. Clark was an inspiration to young players everywhere. It will be fun to see what she can do next!

Men's Tournament

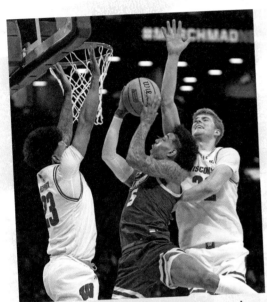

Purple power: JMU shocked Wisconsin.

HAPPENS EVERY YEAR

Well, it sure seems like it, right? People filling out brackets always look for the 12-vs.-5 matchup, because at least one seems to be an upset each season. In 2024, it was James Madison shocking 5-seed Wisconsin 72-61. Defense was the key, as JMU forced 19 Wisconsin turnovers. No. 12-seed Grand Canyon made it a twofer by beating 5-seed St. Mary's 75-66. Bonus: It was GCU's first NCAA tournament victory ever!

FIGHT ON, BULLDOGS!

The Ivy League has some of the most famous schools in the world, but it rarely has super sports teams. Tell that to 13-seed Yale, which shocked SEC Tournament champ Auburn 78-76. Yale trailed by 10 points in the second half before rallying to upset Auburn, busting brackets around the country!

GRRRRIZZLIES!

The Golden Grizzlies of Oakland (Michigan) punched their ticket to the dance for the first time since 2011. They made the trip memorable by pulling off the biggest upset of the event: 14-seed Oakland beat 3-seed Kentucky 80-76. Oakland's **Jack Gohlke** became this year's fan favorite, after admitting he knew that Kentucky had future draft picks on their team and he had no future in the NBA. That didn't stop Gohlke from dropping 32 points on Kentucky, thanks to the 10 three-point shots he buried. (Fun trivia: Gohlke took 347 three-point shots in the 2023–24 regular season. He took only 8 two-point shots!)

Hard-charging Sears (right) led the way as Alabama beat Clemson to earn a Final Four bid.

WOLVES RUN IN PACKS!

Sports fans love patterns. In 2023, underdog University of Miami saw both their men's and women's teams make runs to the Elite Eight. In 2024, underdog NC State saw both their men's and women's teams make it to the Final Four. On the men's side, the 11-seed Wolfpack put themselves on the map by defeating the 4-seed Duke 76-64. That sent NC State to their first Final Four since 1983. The school was also only the seventh double-digit seed ever to make it to the national semifinals.

SOUTHERN SURPRISE II

The Wolfpack wasn't the only team making history. Alabama rolled to its first Final Four trip after the Crimson Tide defeated Clemson 89-82. 'Bama went longball to win, pouring in 16 three-point shots, including a team-high 7 by Mark Sears. The team's win was even more impressive when you learn they *missed* its first 12 of 13 three-pointers. But they stuck with the strategy, and it paid off. Incredibly, Clemson had only let opponents make 14 threes combined in its first three tournament games!

Men's Final Four
NATIONAL SEMIFINALS

Purdue 63, North Carolina State 50

NC State basketball fans had a fantastic March. Both their men's and women's teams were underdogs, but both reached the national semifinals. In this game, Purdue had no interest in letting an 11-seed reach the title game. Purdue advanced to their first national championship since 1969 after a 13-point win over the Wolfpack. After losing to 16-seed Fairleigh Dickinson in the first round in 2023, Purdue's comeback story was completed thanks to the play of Zach Edey, who collected 20 points and 12 rebounds.

Castle was the king in a big UConn victory.

Big men battle: Zach Edey vs. D.J. Burns Jr.

Connecticut 86, Alabama 72

The fact that the 14-point difference in score was UConn's closest game in the NCAA tournament tells you all you need to know about this Huskies team. Freshman Stephon Castle was the headliner in this game. He scored a career-high 21 points to send the Huskies to their sixth national title game. Dating back to 2023, UConn's win in the national semi was their 11th in a row in NCAA tournament play. Even more impressive, every single one of those games was won by double digits. It was a win of sorts for Alabama, which reached the first Final Four in school history.

Championship Game

Connecticut 75, Purdue 60

There was just no stopping UConn this year. The Huskies won all their NCAA tournament games by at least 10 points while defending their 2023 championship. UConn became only the third program in the last 50 years to win back-to-back national championships (Florida in 2006 and 2007 and Duke in 1991 and 1992).

Tristen Newton was named the Final Four's Most Outstanding Player. The fifth-year senior became the first ever to have 20 points, 5 rebounds, and 5 assists in the title game without committing a turnover.

The game itself did not involve much drama, with the Huskies taking a six-point lead into halftime.

They pushed it to double digits early in the second half. For Purdue, their quest to win the school's first national championship will have to wait at least one more season.

A couple notes to cap off the men's tournament: For Purdue, the title game was their first loss all season to a nationally-ranked team, after coming to the night a perfect 11–0. UConn became the first No. 1 overall seed to win the tournament in 11 years.

In 2024–25, UConn will attempt to pull off the first three-peat since coach **John Wooden**'s UCLA Bruins won an incredible seven championships in a row between 1967 and 1973.

The Huskies grabbed another trophy for their already-full case!

Women's Tournament

Bryanna Brady led Presbyterian to the W.

FIRST TIMER: The First Four is always fun to keep an eye on. Four teams are chosen to play two games, with the winners earning the final spots in the full NCAA tournament. In 2024, one of those games was special. Presbyterian, a school in South Carolina, won the Big South Championship. That gave them a First Four spot, and they made the most of it, beating Connecticut's Sacred Heart 49-42 for the program's first-ever Division I NCAA tournament win. Though they lost to eventual champ South Carolina by 52 points in the next game, it was a memorable March for the Blue Hose (that's their nickname).

RARE UPSETS: Once the regular tournament began, there were fewer upsets than in the men's brackets. The only first-round high seed to win was 11-seed Middle Tennessee. They surprised 6-seed Louisville 71-69. In the second round, 7-seed Duke kept 2-seed Ohio State out of the Sweet Sixteen. Duke was down by as much as 16 points before rallying for the 75-63 win. It helps to have a head coach like Kara Lawson, who is not only a former WNBA champ but an Olympic gold medalist!

THE REMATCH: In 2023, LSU vs. Iowa drew nearly 10 million TV viewers for the national championship game. A year later, with the Caitlin Clark show reaching its full potential and a trip to the Final Four on the line, that record was beaten. More than 12.3 million viewers tuned in to see if Clark and the Hawkeyes could

MOST WOMEN'S FINAL FOURS
(Through 2024)

SCHOOL	FINAL FOURS
Connecticut	23
Tennessee	18
Stanford	15
Louisiana Tech	10
Notre Dame	9

North Carolina State players took a joyful swim in the confetti after a big win.

Clark and Reese put on quite a show.

spoil the Tigers' attempt to repeat. Clark led Iowa to a big victory with 41 points, 12 assists, and 7 rebounds. Clark set the record for Division I career NCAA tournament three-pointers and assists. Iowa outlasted LSU 94-87. In her final game as a Tiger, superstar Angel Reese scored 17 points to go along with 20 rebounds.

WHO'S LEFT?: Joining Iowa in the Final Four
was top-seeded South Carolina, trying to complete a perfect season. Powerhouse UConn made it to its 23rd Final Four, hoping to add to its record total of 11 national titles. The surprise member of this Final Four was North Carolina State. The Wolfpack punched its ticket to the Final Four for the first time since 1998 after defeating 1-seed Texas 76-66. NC State did not even win the ACC Tournament but beat Texas and 2-seed Stanford on its amazing run.

Women's Final Four
NATIONAL SEMIFINALS

Iowa 71,
Connecticut 69

It came down to 40 seconds of hold-your-breath defense for the Hawkeyes, but in the end, Iowa got the job done to advance to the national championship game for the second straight season. Caitlin Clark helped with 21 points. The Huskies did lead by as many as 12 during the first half, but a steady surge by the Hawkeyes proved to be too much. Iowa defeated Connecticut for the first time in 33 seasons to return to the title game.

South Carolina 78,
North Carolina State 59

You won't be able to tell by the final score, but this was actually a one-point game at halftime. The problem for NC State? South Carolina outscored them 29-6 in the third quarter. Kamilla Cardoso dropped 22 points and grabbed 11 rebounds in only 23 minutes of play. Ashlyn Watkins collected 20 rebounds in a dominant showing for SC. The 23-point margin in that third quarter was the largest single-quarter margin in Final Four history.

All-around play by Watkins (left) was key to South Carolina's semifinal win.

National Championship

South Carolina 87, Iowa 75

After falling to Iowa in the Final Four in 2023, South Carolina took out their frustrations on the entire NCAA. They capped a perfect 38–0 season with an 87-75 win over Iowa in the national championship game. Coach Dawn Staley's team became only the 10th Division I women's team to complete a perfect season, and the first since Connecticut in 2016.

For the Gamecocks, the championship was their second in the last three years, and third in the last eight. With her third title, Staley became only the fifth coach to win at least three national titles.

Kamilla Cardoso, who was named the Final Four's Most Outstanding Player, capped off her great season with 15 points and 17 rebounds. Headlined by freshman Tessa Johnson's 19 points, the Gamecocks bench outscored Iowa's 37-0!

Iowa star Caitlin Clark did all she could in her final game, leading the game's scorers with 30 points. However, Clark's trailblazing journey ended in a national championship loss for the second season in a row.

Bad news for everyone else in the NCAA: South Carolina graduated only three of their 12 players, meaning they have a chance to go

Cardoso was the tournament MOP!

for three in 2025. Perhaps the biggest winner of this season, though? The sport of women's basketball. More than 18.9 million people tuned into the national championship, one of the biggest audiences in women's sports history. You'll be seeing it on T-shirts for years to come: Everyone Watches Women's Sports.

ICE HOCKEY

PANTHERS POWER!

You might not think that sunny Florida is a great place to play chilly ice hockey. In June, the Florida Panthers proved you wrong! They won their first Stanley Cup, defeating the Edmonton Oilers in seven thrilling games to become NHL champs. The Oilers nearly pulled off a historic comeback, but the Panthers held on by their claws. The games capped off an exciting 2023–24 season. Read on for all the pro hockey action!

A NEW LEAGUE STARTS!
Congrats to the PWHL, which played its first season of women's pro hockey in 2024. The team from Minnesota was the first champion; read all about their amazing run, starting on page 126! Captain Kendall Coyne Schofield hoisted the Walter Cup!

NHL 2023-24

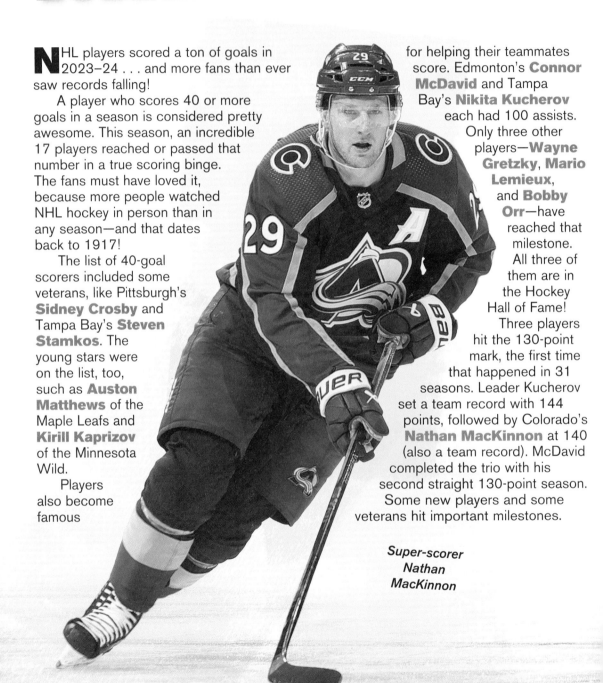

NHL players scored a ton of goals in 2023–24 . . . and more fans than ever saw records falling!

A player who scores 40 or more goals in a season is considered pretty awesome. This season, an incredible 17 players reached or passed that number in a true scoring binge. The fans must have loved it, because more people watched NHL hockey in person than in any season—and that dates back to 1917!

The list of 40-goal scorers included some veterans, like Pittsburgh's **Sidney Crosby** and Tampa Bay's **Steven Stamkos**. The young stars were on the list, too, such as **Auston Matthews** of the Maple Leafs and **Kirill Kaprizov** of the Minnesota Wild.

Players also become famous for helping their teammates score. Edmonton's **Connor McDavid** and Tampa Bay's **Nikita Kucherov** each had 100 assists. Only three other players—**Wayne Gretzky**, **Mario Lemieux**, and **Bobby Orr**—have reached that milestone. All three of them are in the Hockey Hall of Fame!

Three players hit the 130-point mark, the first time that happened in 31 seasons. Leader Kucherov set a team record with 144 points, followed by Colorado's **Nathan MacKinnon** at 140 (also a team record). McDavid completed the trio with his second straight 130-point season. Some new players and some veterans hit important milestones.

Super-scorer Nathan MacKinnon

Quick became "America's Goalie"!

the Lightning. At age 18, that made Bedard the youngest rookie to record a four-point game since 1944! He finished the season with 22 goals and 61 points in 68 games, leading all NHL rookies.

As for the big story among the teams, the Edmonton Oilers, who were loaded with high scorers, just couldn't get going at the start of the season. In November, they had won only three games and lost 10. They fired their head coach, **Jay Woodcroft**, and brought in **Kris Knoblauch**. Knoblauch was head coach of the Rangers' minor league team and had no NHL head-coaching experience. At Christmas, Edmonton was 18 points out of first place in the Pacific Division and slowly clawing their way up. In June, they were playing for the Stanley Cup. That's hockey, fans!

In October 2023, Matthews had hat tricks in his first two games of the season. Only four other players have managed that feat. And only one (**Alex Ovechkin** of the Capitals) did it after 1917. Ovechkin reached his own milestone that month, scoring his 300th power-play goal. No other NHL player has come within 25 goals of that record (he reached 312 by the end of the season).

A couple of New York Rangers hit some high points. Backup goalie **Jonathan Quick** notched his 392nd win in March 2024, becoming the American-born goaltender with the most wins. Rangers center **Matt Rempe** made his debut against the New York Islanders in February 2024, becoming the first NHL player to start his career in an outdoor game. Say what? Well, the game was played at MetLife Stadium, outdoors, where the NFL usually plays.

Another rookie, **Connor Bedard**, scored his first NHL goal in the first period of his first game for the Chicago Blackhawks. On November 9, he got two goals and two assists in a 5-3 win against

2023–24 FINAL STANDINGS

EASTERN CONFERENCE		WESTERN CONFERENCE	
RANGERS	114	STARS	113
HURRICANES	111	JETS	110
PANTHERS	110	CANUCKS	109
BRUINS	109	AVALANCHE	107
MAPLE LEAFS	102	OILERS	104
LIGHTNING	98	PREDATORS	99
ISLANDERS	94	KINGS	99
CAPITALS	91	GOLDEN KNIGHTS	98
RED WINGS	91	BLUES	92
PENGUINS	88	WILD	87
FLYERS	87	FLAMES	81
SABRES	84	KRAKEN	81
DEVILS	81	COYOTES	77
SENATORS	78	DUCKS	59
CANADIENS	76	BLACKHAWKS	52
BLUE JACKETS	66	SHARKS	47

Stanley Cup Playoffs

Competition for the Stanley Cup promised to be fiercer than ever. Of the 16 teams to qualify, 10 had more than 100 points during the regular season. Here are some highlights.

In the first round, the Boston Bruins and Toronto Maple Leafs needed all seven games, plus overtime in the seventh! Boston won on a **David Pastrňák** goal. In the West, there would be no repeat for the defending Stanley Cup champion Las Vegas Golden Knights. The Dallas Stars, led by rising star **Wyatt Johnston** and goaltender **Jake Oettinger**, skated to a seven-game victory.

In the second round, the New York Rangers had to hold off the tough Carolina Hurricanes. New York was up 3–0 but let Carolina win a pair of games. In Game 6, down by two goals in the third period, Rangers forward **Chris Kreider** scored three goals in a row to clinch the series. That made Rangers the first winner of the Presidents' Trophy (for most points in the season) to advance to the conference final since 2015.

Also in the second round, the Florida Panthers kept the Bruins trapped in their own end of the ice, shutting down their top scorers.

Can you spot the puck? Hint . . . it's just barely in the goal, thanks to Chris Kreider (in white).

The Panthers got sharp goaltending from **Sergei Bobrovsky** and timely scoring from forward **Evan Rodrigues** to win the series in six games.

In the West, the Vancouver Canucks and Edmonton Oilers were the only Canadian teams left in the playoffs and faced each other. The Canucks took the series lead three times, but the Oilers always answered. **Connor McDavid** helped the Oilers tie the series with three assists in Game 6. In Game 7, the Oilers scored three second-period goals and fought off a Canucks rally to hold on for the series victory.

McDavid led the way for Edmonton.

EASTERN CONFERENCE FINAL

PANTHERS 4, RANGERS 2

The Panthers' swarming checking style and the Rangers' high-powered offense collided. The series also featured two top Russian goaltenders, Bobrovsky and **Igor Shesterkin**. Florida's Bobrovsky notched a shutout in Game 1. That set the tone for the series. The Rangers were constantly trapped in their own end, turned over the puck, and were powerless on the power play. The Rangers did manage to take a 2–1 series lead in the series thanks to the tremendous play of Shesterkin. But the bigger, stronger Panthers clawed their way back into the series when forward **Sam Reinhart** snapped home a game-winning overtime goal in Game 4. The Panthers won the next two games and headed to the Stanley Cup Final.

WESTERN CONFERENCE FINAL

OILERS 4, STARS 2

Edmonton's McDavid tipped home a slick pass from defenseman **Evan Bouchard** in the second overtime of Game 1 to set the Oilers on their way. The Dallas Stars reeled off the next two wins, with veteran captain **Jamie Benn** getting a goal and an assist in Game 2. Dallas's **Jason Robertson** had a hat trick in Game 3. Trailing by two goals in Game 4, the Oilers exploded for five unanswered goals to even the series. They won the next two games to make it to their first Final since 2006.

Stanley Cup Final

GAME ONE

Panthers 3, Oilers 0

The Florida Panthers shut down the Edmonton Oilers' top players. Oilers captain **Connor McDavid** did not have a point for the first time in five games, and the power play was scoreless. They didn't score at even strength, either, as Panthers goalie **Sergei Bobrovsky** turned aside 32 shots.

GAME TWO

Panthers 4, Oilers 1

The unlikely hero was Panthers forward **Evan Rodrigues**. He scored two third-period goals to send the Panthers to a win.

Bobrovsky snares another save for Florida.

The Oilers' power play was shut down again, and they couldn't control the Panthers' offensive attacks. After two games, the Oilers had scored only one goal.

GAME THREE

Panthers 4, Oilers 3

As the series moved to Edmonton, the Panthers sharpened their claws. They scored three second-period goals. Captain **Aleksander Barkov** and forward **Sam Reinhart** each scored a goal and an assist. But then the Oilers had two third-period goals to cut the Panthers' lead. They could do no better, and the Panthers won this very close game.

GAME FOUR

Oilers 8, Panthers 1

Edmonton started an amazing comeback with a big win. McDavid scored his first goal of the series and added three assists to bust **Wayne Gretzky**'s NHL record for assists (31) in a single playoff season. Top Oilers scorers **Leon Draisaitl**, **Zach Hyman**, and **Ryan Nugent-Hopkins** each got their first points of the series in the lopsided win.

GAME FIVE

Oilers 5, Panthers 3

McDavid and the Oilers kept the comeback going in front of a stunned Florida crowd. McDavid had his second four-point game, making him the first player in NHL history

Spot the puck, part 2: Reinhart (13) slipped in this winning goal in Game 7.

to have back-to-back four-point games in the Stanley Cup Final. Oilers special teams led the way, with a shorthanded goal by **Connor Brown** and power-play goals by Hyman and **Corey Perry**.

Oilers 5, Panthers 1

Everyone was asking: Could the Oilers push this series all the way to Game 7? They gave their hometown fans one to remember, winning 5-1. Each of the Oilers' four lines scored. The Oilers' penalty killers declawed the Panthers, holding them to one goal in 19 tries in the series. **Ryan McLeod** and defenseman **Darnell Nurse** scored empty-net goals for the Oilers to seal the victory. They became the first team since the 1945 Detroit Red Wings to force a Game 7 after trailing three games to none.

Panthers 2, Oilers 1

The 1945 Red Wings did not win their Game 7. The 2024 Oilers didn't, either. The game was tied 1-1 at the end of the first period. Reinhart scored for the Panthers in the second period, and despite a mighty effort by the Oilers, that's how the score remained when the game ended. The Panthers got their first Stanley Cup in team history. McDavid won the Conn Smythe Trophy for best performance throughout the playoffs. It's rare for a player from the losing team to win—it's only happened six times in NHL history.

2023-24 NHL Leaders

144 POINTS
Nikita Kucherov, Lightning ▶ ▶ ▶

69 GOALS
Auston Matthews, Maple Leafs

100 ASSISTS
Connor McDavid, Oilers
Nikita Kucherov, Lightning

92 POINTS (DEFENSE)
Quinn Hughes, Canucks

+56 PLUS-MINUS
Gustav Forsling, Panthers

2.03 GOALS AGAINST AVG.
.925 SAVE PCT.
Anthony Stolarz, Panthers

"There are guys in this league, you put them on the ice, no matter who they're with, and they make everybody better. That's Nikita."

−Tampa Bay coach Jon Cooper

2024 NHL Awards

Hart Trophy
MOST VALUABLE PLAYER
NATHAN MACKINNON, AVALANCHE

Vezina Trophy
TOP GOALTENDER
CONNOR HELLEBUYCK, JETS

James Norris Trophy
TOP DEFENSEMAN
QUINN HUGHES, CANUCKS

Ted Lindsay Award
MOST OUTSTANDING PLAYER,
VOTED BY THE NHL PLAYERS' ASSOCIATION
NATHAN MACKINNON, AVALANCHE

Calder Memorial Trophy
ROOKIE OF THE YEAR
CONNOR BEDARD, BLACKHAWKS ▶▶▶

Lady Byng Trophy
SPORTSMANSHIP
JACCOB SLAVIN, HURRICANES

**Mark Messier
NHL Leadership Award**
JACOB TROUBA, RANGERS

Jack Adams Award
COACH OF THE YEAR
RICK TOCCHET, CANUCKS

PWHL 2024

Montreal and Toronto set PWHL attendance records.

Women's hockey is growing! A new organization, the Professional Women's Hockey League (PWHL), played its first game January 1, 2024. The PWHL has its own Original Six (just like the NHL): Boston, Minnesota, Montreal, New York, Ottawa, and Toronto. The teams don't yet have names and logos; the PWHL put off those major decisions until next season.

Each team played 24 games—including at least four head-to-head meetings with every other team. PWHL players also skated in a three-on-three showcase during the NHL All-Star weekend in Toronto in February.

With four female GMs and three female head coaches, women are getting a chance to take over the top spots in hockey in the PWHL.

The new league's first game took place when Toronto hosted New York. New York's **Ella Shelton** scored the league's first goal, and New York took home the 4-0 win. That game's Canadian television audience of 2.9 million viewers was the largest for any game broadcast that day, beating out the NHL Winter Classic. Fans tuned in to watch fast, physical hockey played with skill and passion.

Several games set attendance records for women's ice hockey. On February 16, Toronto hosted its first game against

NEW RULES

The PWHL rules are a little different from the men's game. Teams get three points for a regulation win, two points for an overtime win, and one point for an overtime loss. A power play ends if the penalized team scores a shorthanded goal. Shootouts after a tie game are best of five (the NHL is best of three). And, at the request of the PWHL players (and unlike in international women's hockey), body checking is allowed.

PWHL LEADERS

27 POINTS
20 GOALS
NATALIE SPOONER, TORONTO ▶▶▶

15 ASSISTS
ALEX CARPENTER, NEW YORK
EMMA MALTAIS, TORONTO

+15 PLUS-MINUS
SUSANNA TAPANI, BOSTON

1.61 GOALS AGAINST
AVERAGE
ELAINE CHULI, MONTREAL

0.949 SAVE PCT.
ELAINE CHULI, MONTREAL

2024 AWARDS

BILLIE JEAN KING MVP AWARD
AND FORWARD OF THE YEAR
Natalie Spooner, TORONTO

DEFENDER OF THE YEAR
Erin Ambrose, MONTREAL

GOALTENDER OF THE YEAR
Kristen Campbell, TORONTO

ROOKIE OF THE YEAR
Grace Zumwinkle, MINNESOTA

COACH OF THE YEAR
Troy Ryan, TORONTO

HOCKEY FOR ALL AWARD
Maureen Murphy, MONTREAL

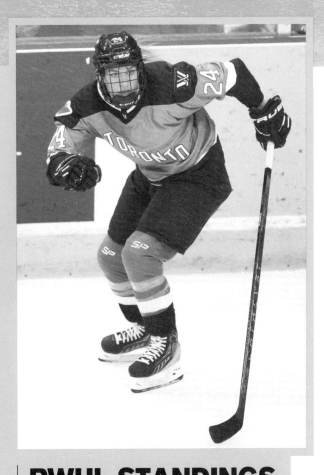

PWHL STANDINGS

TEAM	POINTS
TORONTO	47
MONTREAL	41
BOSTON	35
MINNESOTA	35
OTTAWA	32
NEW YORK	26

Montreal. The sellout crowd of 19,285 set a new all-time high. It didn't last! On April 20, Montreal hosted Toronto and broke the attendance record with 21,105 fans!

While Montreal and New York got out to fast starts, as the season progressed, Toronto and Minnesota came on strong. It became clear that Toronto had a golden goalie in **Kristen Campbell** and a top goalscorer in **Natalie Spooner**. They finished the regular season on top. But the playoffs told a different story! All in all, it was an exciting first season; look for more PWHL action in 2025!

Tapani (right) bangs in one of her two game-winning overtime goals.

PWHL Playoffs

The NHL has Stanley. The PWHL has Walter . . . Cup, that is! The trophy is named for the family that put up nearly all the money to start the PWHL! To see who would get the first Walter Cup, the top four teams entered a two-round playoff tournament. In a PWHL playoff twist, top-finisher Toronto got to pick their opponent. They chose fourth-place Minnesota, which was coming off a five-game losing streak. Toronto had beaten Minnesota in three of their four regular-season matchups.

The best-of-five series featured the PWHL's two stingiest teams. Toronto gave up just 50 goals over the 24-game season, while Minnesota gave up 54. Toronto won the first two games

of the series, and Minnesota did not score a single goal. Then Minnesota shut out Toronto in the next two games. The Game 5 decider was all Minnesota, 4-1. **Taylor Heise** scored the game-winner on the power play 8:30 into the third period.

In the other series, Boston swept Montreal in three very close games, all of which went to overtime. Boston's **Susanna Tapani** scored only two goals in the series, but both were OT game-winners. Game 2 was decided in the third overtime period, with **Taylor Wenczkowski** netting her first career PWHL goal. Boston goalie **Aerin Frankel** made 56 saves in that game, breaking the save record she set in Game 1.

Walter Cup Final

Minnesota 3, Boston 2

The first Walter Cup set a high standard, including great action and a surprise champion.

Minnesota and Boston faced off in a five-game series. Minnesota's **Michela Cava** struck first in Game 1, but at the final buzzer, **Aerin Frankel** stopped 30 of the 33 shots, and Boston won, 4-3.

Minnesota goalie **Nicole Hensley** responded in Game 2 with a shutout. Teammate **Sophie Jaques** had two goals in the 3-0 win.

It was **Taylor Heise**'s turn to be the hero in Game 3. She scored her league-leading fifth playoff goal as part of a 4-1 Minnesota win.

Game 4 was scoreless into two overtime periods. With 2:34 left in the second OT, Jaques had what she thought was the game-winner. The team celebrated on the ice . . . but after a video replay, the goal was disallowed for goaltender interference. A little more than a minute later, Boston's **Alina Muller** scored to send the series to Game 5.

In the clinching game, Hensley notched another shutout, knocking aside 17 shots on goal. Minnesota went up by two, then captain **Kendall Coyne Schofield** scored an empty-net goal to seal the 3-0 victory.

Heise of Minnesota was named the first Ilana Kloss Playoff MVP, after leading the playoffs with five goals, and finishing tied for first in points, with eight.

Heise's scoring was key to Minnesota's championship.

SOCCER

BLACK FUTURE CO OP FUND

GO, GO, GOTHAM!
Gotham FC won its first National Women's Soccer League (NWSL) championship in 2023, defeating OL Reign. Like Gotham's Maitane López Millán (right), Gotham rose above the Reign (and Rose Lavelle) to become a surprise champ. Read on for more about the best NWSL season ever!

CREW CRUISES

Columbus won its fourth Major League Soccer (MLS) title in four seasons in 2023. LAFC and Carlos Vela (right) tried to go back-to-back, but Columbus and Rudy Camacho (left) got out to a two-goal lead, and the defending champs could not catch up. MLS had a terrific 2023; read all about it starting on page 136!

NWSL 2023

The big news for NWSL came before the first game, when the league announced that it was adding two more teams. For the 2024 season, the league will welcome the Utah Royals and a team based near San Francisco named Bay FC. The good news for the league continued in 2023. Attendance was up by 32 percent. Also, more people watched the NWSL on TV than ever; the number of viewers rose by 40 percent! As the season ended, NWSL signed a big new TV deal, promising more growth and more ways for fans to tune in.

On the field, the defending champs, the Portland Thorns, got off to a hot start, winning or tying its first five games. Meanwhile, its opponent in the 2022 championship game, the Kansas City Current, struggled early, dropping three of five.

Young players had a big role in 2023, led by **Alyssa Thompson**, 18, who scored in her first game for Angel City FC. She was not alone. A new rule allowed players younger than 18. Six teenagers were in NWSL in 2023. At just 15, **Melanie Barcenas** of the San Diego Wave set a record as the youngest NWSL player ever.

The race for playoff spots was tight most of the season. At one point in mid-July, the top five teams were separated by only two points. North Carolina and Portland continued their solid runs, while Gotham FC and OL Reign returned to the championship chase. The Reign ended up clinching on the final day thanks to two goals from

Alyssa Thompson

Megan Rapinoe, the US national-team star playing in her final season (see page 135).

San Diego was led again by US team star **Alex Morgan**. In only their second season, the Wave ended up with the best regular-season record. The other second-year team, Angel City, continued to improve, though the team struggled until late in the season. But then Angel City added a new coach. In her first 10 games, **Becki Tweed** was undefeated at 7–0–3 in league and Cup play. In the season's final game, **Sydney Leroux** scored a miracle bicycle kick to help push the team into the playoffs.

Once the playoffs started, the strongest teams stepped up and powered through, setting up a dramatic NWSL championship game.

CHALLENGE CUP

Like many soccer leagues around the world, the NWSL has a separate, in-season Cup competition. Teams play in knockout rounds to reach a championship pairing. In the 2023 title game, the North Carolina Courage made it back-to-back Cup wins, led again by goal-scorer **Kerolin Nicoli**. The Courage beat Racing Louisville 2-0.

2023 NWSL AWARDS

MOST VALUABLE PLAYER
Kerolin Nicoli ▶▶▶
NORTH CAROLINA

DEFENDER OF THE YEAR
Naomi Girma
SAN DIEGO

ROOKIE OF THE YEAR
Jenna Nighswonger
GOTHAM FC

GOALKEEPER OF THE YEAR
Jane Campbell
HOUSTON

COACH OF THE YEAR
Juan Carlos Amorós
GOTHAM FC

NWSL Playoffs

FIRST ROUND

Angel City's late-season run ended with a 1-0 loss to OL Reign in **Megan Rapinoe**'s final home game with the Reign. Gotham FC won its first-ever playoff game, knocking off the NC Courage 2-0.

SEMIFINALS

A pair of surprise teams earned chances to play for the NWSL title. **Katie Stengel** scored a 107th-minute goal as Gotham FC beat defending champion Portland. The game was played in pouring rain in Portland, and the powerful Thorns just could not find a goal. In the other semi, San Diego came in as the top seed but were upset 1-0 by OL Reign. That team is led by US national-team star Rapinoe, who announced her retirement. So her last game was to play for the NWSL championship!

NWSL Championship Game, here we come . . . thanks to this goal by Stengel.

Championship

Gotham 2, Reign 1

Gotham FC had finished the 2022 NWSL season in last place. In 2023, in the biggest turnaround in league history, Gotham stormed to the team's first title with a 2-1 win in the championship game. Forward **Midge Purce** was the star; she had assists on both of the team's goals, one by **Lynn Williams** and the clincher by **Esther González**. Gotham lost its goalie late in the game to a red card, so midfielder **Nealy Martin** had to step in. But the Reign could not score again, and Gotham took home the title. Purce was named the championship game MVP. The game was also the last in the great careers of US Women's National Team stars **Megan Rapinoe** (box) and **Ali Krieger**. Krieger added this trophy to her two Women's World Cup titles.

Let the confetti fly! Gotham is the champ!

THANKS, MEGAN!

Megan Rapinoe did not want her amazing career to end this way. She had to leave the NWSL championship game after only a few minutes when she injured her Achilles tendon. She limped off into history as one of the best American players ever. Rapinoe had led the US team to two World Cup titles. In the 2019 win, she was named the top player in the tournament and later was named World Player of the Year. Her leadership on and off the field will be hard to replace, but she inspired millions of young players everywhere.

MLS 2023

Lionel Messi

> "The eyes of the world are now on Major League Soccer because the best player to ever play the game is here and he's succeeding."
>
> — MLS COMMISSIONER **DON GARBER**

By far the biggest news in MLS 2023 (or even in American sports!) came in June, when Argentina's superstar **Lionel Messi** announced he was joining Inter Miami. He becomes probably the biggest name ever in MLS history (perhaps tied with **David Beckham** . . . a team owner in Miami!). In his first game with his new team, Messi thrilled his worldwide fans by knocking in a game-winning free kick in the final minute! It just kept getting better for Miami, which was in last place when the Argentine star showed up. He scored two goals in each of his first three games. Miami won the new Leagues Cup over first-place FC Cincinnati. In the US Open Cup, they reached the final but lost to Houston.

Messi was a worldwide story. Tickets to his games went for thousands of dollars. The Miami team Instagram went from one million followers to 15 million! Stores could not keep his pink No. 10 shirt in stock.

Miami didn't end up making the playoffs, but the "Messi Effect" surely continued in 2024. He was part of the MLS's most successful season ever, with a record 11 million people seeing games in person. The Apple TV

Acosta powered the Cincinnati attack.

the league leaders, helped by former MVP **Carles Gil** steering New England's offense.

But all those teams were chasing surprising FC Cincinnati, which won the Supporters' Shield with the best regular-season record. It was the first time atop the table for the five-year-old team, which has had some really bad seasons! A key reason for 2023's success was Argentine star **Luciano Acosta**, who was named the league MVP.

A big highlight for MLS came on July 4, when a new MLS attendance record was set. At the El Trafico rivalry game between LAFC and the LA Galaxy, 82,110 people packed the Rose Bowl in Pasadena. The Galaxy won 2-1.

The playoffs thrilled fans with close calls and epic comebacks. Read on to find out how the champs ended up on top!

deal brought millions more eyeballs to MLS games in 2023 as well.

Hidden by the Messi news was an incredible story in St. Louis. In its first season, the city's new team set a record by winning its first five games. It won six of its first 10 and led the Western Conference. By September, they were still in first place. No team has won an MLS title in its first season (since the league's first season in 1996, of course!).

They were chased by Seattle, a former champ led by US star **Jordan Morris**. Defending champ LAFC was in the hunt, too. Rising star **Dénis Bouanga** was the MLS scoring leader, joining former MVP **Carlos Vela** to give LA a scoring punch.

In the East, New England rebounded from a tough 2022 season to be among

MLS AWARDS

MOST VALUABLE PLAYER
LUCIANO ACOSTA, Cincinnati

DEFENDER OF THE YEAR
MATT MIAZGA, Cincinnati

GOALKEEPER OF THE YEAR
ROMAN BÜRKI, St. Louis

GOLDEN BOOT (TOP SCORER)
DÉNIS BOUANGA, LAFC

YOUNG PLAYER OF THE YEAR
THIAGO ALMADA, Atlanta

COMEBACK PLAYER OF THE YEAR
ALAN PULIDO, Sporting KC

High-flying Ramirez was the hero of Columbus's Eastern Conference win.

MLS Playoffs

For 2023, MLS used a three-game playoff system for the first round. Teams had to win two out of three games to advance. The semifinals and final were one-game knockouts.

ROUND ONE

Only three of the eight matchups went to the full three games. The big upset was by Sporting Kansas City, which defeated top-seeded St. Louis in two straight games, ending the MLS's newest team's Cinderella season. Houston had the most dramatic win, needing a penalty shootout to clinch its contest over Salt Lake.

CONFERENCE SEMIFINALS

EAST
Cincinnati 1, Philadelphia 0
Columbus 2, Orlando City 0

WEST
Houston 1, Sporting KC 0
LAFC 1, Seattle 0

CONFERENCE FINALS

EAST

Columbus 3, Cincinnati 2
Christian Ramirez scored in the 115th minute to break a tie and send the Crew to the MLS Cup, which it won in 2020. **Diego Rossi** also scored a second-half goal for Columbus, which came back to defeat the team with the 2023's best overall record.

WEST

LAFC 2, Houston 0
LAFC returned to its second straight MLS Cup with a hard-fought win over a tough Dynamo team. **Ryan Hollingshead** scored late in the first half, and Houston hurt itself with an own goal late in the second half.

MLS Cup 2023

Columbus 2, LAFC 1

Yeboah leaps after scoring a key goal.

when **Diego Palacios** had the ball bounce off his arm in the penalty box. The Crew's **Cucho Hernández** buried the penalty kick to put Columbus on top. That broke a scoreless streak of more than 350 minutes for the LAFC defense and goalie **Maxime Crépeau**.

The goal seemed to rattle LAFC, and just four minutes later, Columbus struck again. **Malte Amundsen** drove a perfect pass through the LAFC back line. **Yaw Yeboah** made an excellent run, touched the ball once, then drove it past a diving Crépeau.

LAFC scored late in the second half, thanks to the hustle of **Dénis Bouanga**. After the Crew's **Patrick Schulte** saved Bouanga's first shot, the LAFC star slipped the rebound inside the post. Columbus then put up a defensive wall and held off any late LAFC charges.

Columbus won only 10 games in 2022, so the championship marked an incredible turnaround.

On a rainy night in front of its home fans, the Columbus Crew captured their third MLS Cup and second in four years. MLS celebrated the end of its best season yet with golden confetti flying over the champions.

LAFC was going for back-to-back titles but could not get any offense going. The Crew put a lot of pressure on the LAFC back line throughout the first half. That attack led to the first goal,

From worst to first: Columbus was the 2023 champ.

Champions League 2024

MEN'S

SEMIFINALS:

Borussia Dortmund sent Paris-St. Germain packing in one semifinal. The German team won 1-0 in each of the two games, keeping powerful **Kylian Mbappé** from scoring. **Jordan Sancho** was electric for Dortmund, making great dribbling runs over and over. In the other semi, Real Madrid scored two late goals in the second game to come back and beat Bayern Munich.

CHAMPIONSHIP

Real Madrid 2, Borussia Dortmund 0

The Spanish giants won their 15th European club title—by far the most ever—over a scrappy

Carvajal (in circle) slipped in this goal to help Real Madrid capture the trophy (right).

Bonmati scored in both the semifinal and final to lead Barcelona to the title.

German team. The game was scoreless through the first half. Dortmund had several good chances, including seven good shots on goal, but could not get past Real goalie **Thibaut Courtois**. Finally, in the 74th minute, **Dani Carvajal** flicked a header in for Madrid. A few minutes later, a bad Dortmund pass led to a goal by superstar **Vinicius Junior**.

WOMEN'S
SEMIFINALS:

In the first semi, Chelsea took a 1-0 lead over Barcelona after the first game. But in the second game, Barcelona took advantage of its home field. **Aitana Bonmati** scored in the first half. **Fridolina Rolfö** knocked in a goal in the 75th minute that put Barça on top to stay. In the all-French second semifinal,

Lyon was in trouble in the first game. They trailed Paris-St. Germain 2-0 in the second half. But three goals in six minutes just before the end turned things around. Lyon kept up the pressure in the second game, winning 2-1 to advance to the team's 11th Champions League final.

CHAMPIONSHIP
Barcelona 2, Lyon 0

When you've got the women's World Player of the Year, you depend on her to come through. Bonmati did just that, scoring in the 63rd minute. Another Barcelona superstar, **Alexia Putellas**, added a late second goal. Those strikes made Barcelona back-to-back Champions League winners; it was also their third overall. They still trail Lyon's all-time total of eight, however!

2023-24 EPL

There was late-season drama in the Premier League. For a while, four teams looked like they had a shot at the top spot. Then Aston Villa hit a rough spot and fell back a bit. Liverpool made a strong run early and was in first place for several weeks. But a late-season streak of losses and ties left it too many points behind to chase.

Meanwhile, Arsenal was excellent all season, leading the league in goals while allowing the fewest scores. Nearly matching them was the three-time defending champ, Manchester City. Powerhouse striker **Erling Haaland** continued to pile up goals for City; he ended up leading the Premier League (again!) with 27.

On the final Sunday, both teams had a shot at the title, but City's **Phil Foden** (the league Player of the Season) scored in the second minute against West Ham, and City never looked back. Their 3-1 win clinched the championship, while Arsenal fell two points short. City became the first club in English history to win four straight top-league championships.

Foden shows off the form that made him the top player.

WOMEN'S SUPER LEAGUE

For the fifth straight season, Chelsea ended up on top of this important England-based league. They beat Manchester United 6-0 on the final Sunday to clinch the title. It was a great way for coach **Emma Hayes** to leave. She became the new head coach of the US Women's National Team, guiding them to a spot in the Summer Olympics in Paris.

DEUTSCHER FUSSBALLMEISTER 2024

Bayer Leverkusen celebrates a history-making German league championship.

Other Top European Leagues

GERMANY

Finally! For the first time since 2012, a team NOT named Bayern Munich was the men's champ. Bayer Leverkusen clinched the title with five games left. They also set a new European record by going 50 games in a row without a loss (they did tie some—this is soccer, after all!). Bayern Munich's fans did get a championship, however. The club's women's team won its sixth Frauen Bundesliga title with two games left in the season.

SPAIN

Real Madrid has one crowded trophy case! The team won its 36th La Liga championship in 2024. English star **Jude Bellingham** and Brazilian striker **Vinicius Junior** led the way with 23 goals each. Barcelona ran away with the Liga Feminina title, finishing **18 points** ahead of Madrid.

FRANCE

Paris-St. Germain lost in the Champions League semifinals, but at least they took home their tenth French league championship. It was the last for superstar **Kylian Mbappé**, who took his skills to talent-rich Real Madrid in 2024. Meanwhile, Lyon continued to dominate French women's soccer. They won their 17th championship in the past 18 years.

ITALY

How do 20 championships equal only two stars? Because in Italy's Serie A, you get to add a star to the logo on your team jersey for winning 10 titles. Inter Milan earned its second star by getting past rival AC Milan for its 20th league crown. AS Roma won the women's league over Juventus for the second season in a row. The two combined for the past seven titles.

Copa América

This is usually the championship of South American national teams. In 2024, the tournament was played in the United States—a sort of practice for the 2026 World Cup. So, along with the US team, some Central American and Caribbean teams joined in. In the early rounds, **Lionel Messi** got an assist in Argentina's 2-0 win over Canada. It was his 35th all-time Copa appearance, a new record. The biggest surprise team was Venezuela, which shocked Mexico in group play. In fact, Mexico did not advance to the quarterfinals, surprising fans north and south of the border. Plus, Canada, added specially like the US team, made it to the quarterfinals for the first time!

US Goes Home Early!

US 2, Bolivia 0 **Christian Pulisic** curled in a beautiful long-range shot in the third minute. He got an assist on **Folarin Balogun's** goal late in the first half. The US defense never let Bolivia threaten, helping get the team off to a great start.

Panama 2, US 1 A disaster. **Tim Weah** got a red card only 20 minutes into the game for a foolish foul. Down a player, the US went ahead on a Balogun goal, but gave up a tying goal minutes later. A late score by Panama sealed the upset. It was only the third win ever by Panama over the Americans, and put the US in a tough position in the group.

Uruguay 1, US 0 The American team flamed out of the Copa with this loss. A team that probably should have gone on instead went home. The World Cup is just two years away . . . so there is time to get better.

Matt Turner helps Joe Scally after a loss.

SEMIFINALS

ARGENTINA 2, CANADA 0

Canada's surprising run at this tournament ended with a loss to the defending champs. Argentina had already beaten Canada in the group stage and had little problem in this rematch. **Julian Alvarez** scored in the first half, while superstar **Lionel Messi** got the second goal later in the game.

COLOMBIA 1, URUGUAY 0

Even though they had to play one player down for nearly an hour, Colombia held on to beat Uruguay. The great **James Rodriguez** (left) set up **Jefferson Lerma** for a goal in the 39th minute. That gave Rodriguez a tournament-best six assists. Then Colombia defended well enough to shut out Uruguay.

CHAMPIONSHIP GAME

ARGENTINA 1, COLOMBIA 0

Colombia came in on a streak of 28 games with no losses. The streak ended here, with Argentina winning its second straight Copa América. Messi had to watch the end from the bench in tears after an ankle injury. After 90 minutes without a goal, the teams played extra time. In the 112th minute, **Lautaro Martinez** got the game's only score with a strong right-footed shot. The goal made him the tournament's top scorer, and the win gave Argentina 16 Copas, the most ever.

Lautaro Martinez

Euros 2024

The biggest soccer tournament after the World Cup is the European Championship, known by its nickname: the Euros. The top 24 teams gathered in Germany for group play, then a 16-team knockout tournament.

Early Rounds

✱ In the first round of group play, Slovakia beat Belgium 1-0. With Belgium ranked No. 3 and Slovakia No. 48, it was the biggest upset in Euro history. But wait, that record did not last! In the final stage of Group F, No. 74 Georgia beat No. 6 Portugal 2-0! European soccer had a new biggest upset ever! It was also the first time that Georgia had ever played in the tournament!

Bellingham's incredible bicycle goal saved England!

✱ Albania didn't make the final 16, but it did set a record with the fastest goal ever, just 23 seconds into its loss to Italy.

✱ The top scorer in group play? Some guy named Own Goal, who played for many teams. There were a total of 10 OGs knocked in . . . all by accident, of course.

✱ Late goals were another theme. A record nine stoppage-time goals were scored, including a 98th-minute goal by Italy to tie Croatia and knock them out of the tournament. Hungary sent Scotland home with a 100th-minute goal, the latest regular-time score in the Euros.

✱ England needed a miracle bicycle-kick goal from **Jude Bellingham** and an extra-time header by **Harry Kane** to squeak into the quarterfinals over Slovakia 2-1.

✱ Turkish goalie **Mert Gunok** made one of the best saves in years, knocking aside a shot by Austria in the final seconds. That preserved his team's 2-1 win.

Quarterfinals

Spain 2, Germany 1 An 119th-minute goal by **Mikel Merino** knocked out the host nation.

France 0, Portugal 0 France won in a penalty shootout, without star **Kylian Mbappé**.

England 1, Switzerland 1 England goalie **Jordan Pickford**'s save led to a PK-shootout win.

Netherlands 2, Türkiye 1 Netherlands won on a late, game-winning own goal by Türkiye.

Semifinals

Spain 2, France 1
Teenagers rule! After France's **Randal Kolo Muani** scored to take the lead, 16-year-old **Lamine Yamal** rocketed in a tying goal. In Euro and World Cup history, he is now the youngest ever to score! Yamal's teammate **Dani Olmo** scored not long after and Spain held on to win an exciting, action-packed game.

England 2, Netherlands 1
Can they do it? Can England break a curse that has lasted nearly 60 years? The country that invented soccer has not won a major

event since 1966. They have never won the Euros. **Xavi Simons** scored an early goal for the Dutch. **Harry Kane** tied it with a penalty. Then **Ollie Watkins** gave England a chance when he scored in the 90th minute. England held on to return to the championship game.

Championship Game

Spain 2, England 1
Spain completed a perfect 7–0 run at these Euros and earned its fourth title, the most all-time in this famous event. The first half was scoreless. Then Spain's **Nico Williams** opened the scoring with a goal. England got life from **Cole Palmer** late in the second half. But they could not stop the relentless Spanish attack. With just four minutes left until extra time, **Mikel Oyarzabal** poked in a cross past the England goalie for the winning goal.

Oyarzabal (right) had to slide to poke in this goal with his toe!

Africa Cup of Nations

How did Côte d'Ivoire (also known as Ivory Coast) win this important continental championship? You had to see it to believe it. Few teams have beaten the odds like this team, which defeated Nigeria in the championship game 2-1.

Though the tournament was held in its own country, Côte d'Ivoire struggled in the group play, squeaking into the final 16 with the lowest record and losing two games (including one to Nigeria). Then, they were behind in in every one of the knockout games. But somehow, they managed to find a way back to win each time.

Côte d'Ivoire beat Senegal on penalty kicks, then squeaked by DR Congo in the semifinal.

In the title game, Nigeria scored first and put Côte d'Ivoire behind . . . again. No problem! **Franck Kessié** scored in the second half to tie the score.

Sébastien Haller scored the go-ahead goal with less than 10 minutes left in the game. Haller was a one-man comeback story. He had missed most of the early games with an ankle injury.

This is Côte d'Ivoire's third Cup of Nations win; they also won in 1992 and 2015.

Haller (22) rose high for a bicycle kick attempt against Nigeria.

The Qatari team tossed championship-game hero Afif in the air after his three goals.

Asian Cup

The country of Qatar hosted the 2022 World Cup, but didn't win a game. They had better luck in the 2024 Asian Cup, which they also hosted.

The home team won all three of its group-stage games, while not allowing a single goal. They beat Palestine and Uzbekistan in the knockout games, but needed penalties in the second win. In the semifinal, a late goal by **Almoez Ali** gave Qatar a 3-2 win over Iran.

Qatar's opponent in the final was, like Côte d'Ivoire in Africa, a big surprise. After finishing third in group play, Jordan had to score twice in extra time to upset Iraq. Jordan then shocked highly-ranked South Korea to make the championship game.

Their luck ran out, however. Jordan committed three penalties and Qatar's **Akram Afif** buried all three penalty kicks in the back of the net. The 3-1 win gave Qatar back-to-back Asian Cup crowns, the first time that has been done since Japan won in 2000 and 2004.

MOTOR SPORTS

VIVA LAS VEGAS!
Formula 1 returned to Las Vegas for one of the highlights of the 2023 motor sports calendar. Drivers sped past the bright lights of the Strip and past the massive new Sphere (above). For the full story of all the fast-moving racing action, turn the page!

NASCAR 2023

NASCAR celebrated its 75th anniversary in 2023. One of the celebrations added 25 drivers to an earlier all-time top 50. In the 2023 season, fans could watch 10 of those drivers compete in NASCAR! (Okay, it was actually 11—Jimmie Johnson came back for three races.) But in the end, those fans saw a first-time champion.

The season started with an exciting Daytona 500. Ricky Stenhouse Jr. needed double overtime to win his first 500. It was the longest-ever event in the famous race, with 12 extra laps and 30 extra miles. The win was also the first for a team co-owned by a woman (Jodi Geschickter) and a Black person (former NBA hero Brad Daugherty).

Through the end of April, Kyle Larson, William Byron, and Kyle Busch each won two races, setting up a tight battle for the summertime lead.

Running into another car on the freeway is very bad. Running into a car in NASCAR is just another day at the track. At a Kansas race that included 37 lead changes, Denny Hamlin won by bumping Kyle Larson out of the way on the final lap.

The midsummer All-Star Race does not count in the points standings, but a win by Larson paid off big. He won his third All-Star Race in five seasons, which earned him a $1 million bonus!

Larson won an All-Star Race and a check that was big in more ways than one!

As June began, Kyle Busch helped himself by winning a race in St. Louis that included 11 yellow flags for accidents. On the twisting track at Sonoma, California, Martin Truex Jr. won his second race to move into first place overall with 525 points. However, the race at the top was tight: five drivers had 500 points or more.

NASCAR held its first-ever race on the city streets of Chicago in early July. Rain took away some of the excitement. The drivers got only a few practice runs, and the race started late and was shortened due to flooding on the track. The driver who came the farthest to take part ended up winning. New Zealand's Shane van Gisbergen won in his first NASCAR race.

At Pocono Raceway in Pennsylvania, Hamlin won his 50th career NASCAR race. He had to battle Larson down the stretch to win. The regular season ended in a race at Daytona. Ryan Preece survived a scary crash—his car flipped 10 times before landing on the infield grass. Bubba Wallace snagged the final playoff spot with an 12th-place finish. Byron and Truex tied for the points lead heading into the Chase.

The prerace lineup of NASCAR vehicles made for a colorful sight on the streets of Chicago.

Now that's close! Blaney (yellow) squeaked ahead of Harvick to win Talladega.

2023 CHASE FOR THE CUP!

ROUND OF 16

DARLINGTON: Kyle Larson punched the first ticket to the next round. He held off Chris Buescher and Tyler Reddick to win his first Southern 500 at this famous track in South Carolina.

KANSAS: Denny Hamlin led most of the way, but a late caution caused a sudden-death restart. Hamlin was second to Reddick by less than half a second! Hamlin was sort of a winner, though—he co-owns Reddick's race team!

BRISTOL: A crash made Joey Logano the first defending champ to leave a playoff in the first round. He was joined by retiring former champ Kevin Harvick. Hamlin won and earned a spot in the Round of 12.

ROUND OF 12

TEXAS: William Byron won his season-best sixth race to clinch a spot in the next round. The race made Byron's team, Hendrick Motorsports, the first ever to win 300 races all-time.

TALLADEGA: Ryan Blaney punched his ticket to the next round by the thinnest of margins. In this race in Alabama, he beat Harvick by 0.012 seconds. That's about the time it takes to blink your eyes!

Bell waved the checkered flag in Miami.

CHARLOTTE: A.J. Allmendinger waited until this race to earn his first win of the season. Good timing! His road-course victory earned him a spot in the Round of 8. Former champs Brad Keselowski and Kyle Busch were eliminated along with Bubba Wallace and Ross Chastain.

ROUND OF 8

LAS VEGAS: Kyle Larson . . . come on down! Larson earned the first automatic spot in the final four by leading the most laps and, of course, leading at the end. Christopher Bell tried to make it close, but Larson held on for the vital victory.

MIAMI: From out to in—that's what happened to Bell in Miami. Coming into the race, he was not going to have enough points for the final four. He had to win . . . and he did! It was only his second win of the season. That left two spots to fill in the final race in West Virginia.

MARTINSVILLE: The only way Blaney was going to make it into the championship race was to win here. So he did! He was joined by Byron, who had won six races already but needed points in this race to reach the final. By finishing a "lucky" 13th, he squeaked in ahead of Hamlin.

Blaney (No. 12) came through in the clutch, winning in Martinsville to make the final.

Other NASCAR Series

TRUCK SERIES

A long series of crashes and restarts led to 29 laps of overtime. But it was all worth the wait for **Ben Rhodes**, who held on to win his second Truck Series title. Rhodes was in one of the crashes but roared back into the lead pack. As more crashes caused restart after restart, Rhodes stayed ahead of the other three finalists. His fifth-place finish in the race was the highest among the final four. Rhodes had won his first truck title in 2021.

Rhodes after his "rhode" to victory!

XFINITY

The final race in Phoenix needed overtime to determine a winner from the final four drivers aiming for this title, the second-highest in NASCAR. Three of those four were neck and neck on the last laps as fans rose to cheer for their favorites. After some bumping and dodging, **Cole Custer** swooped ahead of **Justin Allgaier**. The car's engines roared as the finish line neared . . . and Custer won, just 0.6 seconds ahead of **Sheldon Creed** and 0.7 ahead of Allgaier. It was Custer's first national championship and third race win of the season.

Custer took the checkered flag!

2023 Championship Race

Thirty-six cars started the final race of the 2023 season, the championship race. But only one of those four drivers could win the season championship. The four were Christoper Bell, Ryan Blaney, William Byron, and Kyle Larson—the drivers who had made it through the playoff chase. In the final in Phoenix, after battling for the lead with 20 laps to go, Blaney charged ahead of the other three finalists. He finished second in the race behind Ross Chastain, but he was the top playoff driver. It was Blaney's first NASCAR championship. It gave owner Roger Penske back-to-back titles and made Ford, Blaney's car company, the champ in all three NASCAR divisions.

Time to celebrate and wave the flag after Blaney won his first NASCAR championship.

Formula 1 2023

From the first start of the 2023 Formula 1 season, it was just about all over. Red Bull's Max Verstappen put on one of the most dominating performances in F1 history. The Dutch driver won an incredible 19 races, including 10 in a row at one point. He won his third straight Formula 1 championship by 290 points over his Red Bull teammate Sergio "Checo" Pérez.

Red Bull roared out of the starting grid in 2023, winning the first 14 races. Verstappen kept up his success from 2022, winning the season opener in Bahrain and then again in Australia. His teammate Pérez won in Saudia Arabia and Baku. Red Bull was so dominant that those two drivers also earned second place in three of those first four races. Seven-time champ Lewis Hamilton managed to grab a second-place finish in Australia. The 2022 season had been a runaway for Verstappen. The 2023 season was looking like a battle for points behind both Red Bull drivers.

A highlight of early races was the appearance of Logan Sargeant. Driving for Williams Racing, the Florida native was the first American to start in Formula 1 since 2015.

A rare cancellation of a race happened in May in Italy. Bad flooding around the racetrack made it unsafe for fans and drivers.

The Red Bull domination continued in Miami as Verstappen roared from ninth to first to win his third race of the season.

The best driver in the best car equaled one of the greatest F1 seasons ever!

Another F1 season trophy for Verstappen

Second place? Pérez, of course! That began a string of six straight wins for Verstappen, including his first British Grand Prix championship in July.

Win No. 7 in Verstappen's streak came at the Hungarian Grand Prix. Hamilton snagged his first pole since 2021, but Verstappen squeaked past on the first lap and led almost the rest of the way. During the victory ceremony, though, second-place finisher Lando Norris knocked over the ceramic trophy, shattering it! Verstappen

earned $70 million in 2023, so he can afford to get a new one!

Later, Verstappen set a new all-time F1 record with his 10th checkered flag in a row as he won the Italian Grand Prix.

The Red Bull streak finally ended in Singapore. Ferrari's Carlos Sainz Jr. became the first non–Red Bull driver to win in 2023. With Norris second and Hamilton third, Red Bull drivers were shut out (but Verstappen stayed *waayyy* ahead in the points race). Order was restored in the next race in Japan, as Verstappen won from the pole.

In a sprint race in Qatar, Verstappen won again, giving him enough points to clinch the title for the third year in a row. He won five more races to set the new single-season record of 19 wins. A big highlight was win No. 18 in the new Las Vegas race. More than 300,000 fans watched the night race under the bright lights of Vegas.

In 2021, Verstappen won his first title on the last lap of the last race. In 2022, he had won by 146 points.

In 2023, he simply blew away the rest of the field. Can Fast Max make it four in a row in 2024?

Verstappen shows how many races he won in a row.

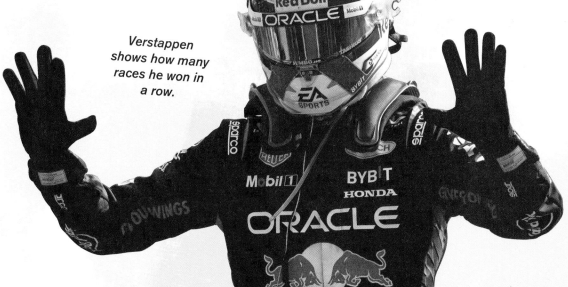

2023 IndyCar

At the start of the 2023 IndyCar season, it looked like the season title was anyone's to grab. Five different drivers sped to victory in the season's first five races, continuing a trend that had started in 2022. One of them, Kyle Kirkwood, took home the checkered flag for the first time in his career. Kirkwood sped to victory on the twisting streets of Long Beach, California. Josef Newgarden was the first two-time winner. He won in Texas and then won his first Indy 500 in May . . . on his 12th try! The fifth of those five drivers was Álex Palou. His May win at the Indianapolis Grand Prix launched him into a year that ended with his second IndyCar season championship. How did he get there?

In June 2023, the city of Detroit roared back onto the Indy calendar. A course was set up through the busy streets, and cars sped beneath skyscrapers and down wide

Champ Palou posed for a selfie with his winning crew.

Newgarden kissed the bricks!

INDY 500 '24

Why is that man kissing bricks? The Indianapolis Motor Speedway is nicknamed "The Brickyard." That's what the original track was made of when it opened in 1909. A single strip of bricks remains, and the Indy 500 winner gets to smooch it. Josef Newgarden puckered up after zipping past Pato O'Ward on the final lap to win his second 500 in a row. O'Ward was only one-third of a second behind! Meanwhile, Newgarden won a $440,000 bonus for becoming the first driver to go back-to-back since Helio Castroneves in 2002.

city boulevards. Palou had been worried that the turns were too tight, but on race day, he must have figured something out. He led 74 of the 100 laps, and took the lead back from Will Power late in the race.

At the Road America course in Wisconsin, Palou won again. Colton Herta led most of the way, but Palou made a big pass with seven laps left. He held off several challengers to win by more than four seconds. Palou remained in first place in points after the first eight races.

At the Mid-Ohio course in July, Palou continued his hot streak, winning to give him four checkered flags out of five races.

Iowa is a two-race weekend, and Newgarden won back-to-back to leap into second place in the standings. He also tied Palou with four wins through late July.

Palou extended his lead in August with a third-place finish in Nashville. In that race,

Kirkwood won his second-ever IndyCar event.

Heading into the second to last event in Portland, Palou held a solid lead in the points race. He told his team owner before the race, "Let's go wrap this up today." Then he did just that, winning his fifth race of the season to clinch the title.

FINAL INDYCAR STANDINGS

DRIVER	POINTS
1. Álex Palou	656
2. Scott Dixon	578
3. Scott McLaughlin	488
4. Pato O'Ward	484
5. Josef Newgarden	479

GOLF

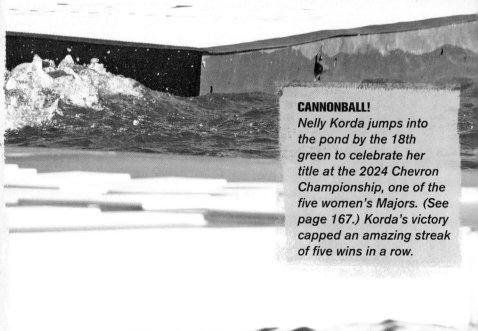

CANNONBALL!
Nelly Korda jumps into the pond by the 18th green to celebrate her title at the 2024 Chevron Championship, one of the five women's Majors. (See page 167.) Korda's victory capped an amazing streak of five wins in a row.

2023 Ryder Cup

To a big golf fan, the Ryder Cup is like the Olympics or the World Cup. It is the most talked-about event on the golf calendar. It comes around only once every two years; a team of golfers from the United States plays a team of golfers from Europe.

The 2023 Ryder Cup was played at a course near Rome, Italy. The United States was the defending champion, having easily won in Wisconsin in 2021. But the US had last won the event in Europe back in 1993.

Europe started strong the first day of the competition and never looked back. With top players such as **Jon Rahm** of Spain and **Rory McIlroy** of Ireland leading the way, the Europeans swept the foursome matches on the morning of the first day. The US team, led by world No. 1–ranked **Scottie Scheffler**, played better in the afternoon four-ball matches but still managed only three ties. For the first time ever, the Americans went winless over an entire day in a Ryder Cup and trailed 6½ points to 1½ points.

On day two, Europe won three of the four foursomes, and the US took three of four four-balls. That left the Americans trailing 10½ to 5½ with only 12 singles matches left to play on the third and final day.

No team had ever rallied from so far down on the last day, but the US gave it a shot. With seven matches left, Europe led 14–7. They needed only half a point more to win the Cup. Then things started turning. The US won four matches in a row. It was 14–11 with three matches still out on the course. There was hope for the Americans after all!

Then suddenly, the hope was gone. England's **Tommy Fleetwood** closed out a win against **Rickie Fowler**, and Europe had won the Cup in Europe again.

Captain Luke Donald (center) and his Ryder Cup winners.

Around the Links

Two golfers had dominant seasons for most of 2024. By June, **Scottie Scheffler** had matched **Tiger Woods**'s great 2009 season. **Nelly Korda** tied a record for most women's tournaments wins in a row! They were part of a great year in golf.

Record Run

After winning four times on the LPGA Tour in 2021 and once in 2022, No. 1–ranked women's player **Nelly Korda** failed to earn a victory in 2023. But in 2024, she bounced back big! Korda won a remarkable five consecutive events. That equaled the LPGA record shared by two legends of the game: **Nancy Lopez** (1978) and **Annika Sorenstam** (2004–05). Korda won events in Florida, California, Arizona, and Las Vegas to set up her biggest win, the Chevron Championship, the first Major of the year. She didn't break the record but did add another win in May, cementing her world No. 1 ranking.

Tiger-Like

When Scheffler won the 2024 Travelers Championship in a playoff, he became the first player to win six times in a single year on the PGA Tour since Woods in 2009—and it was still only June! Scheffler made 12 top-10 finishes in 13 tries. His World Golf Rankings points through June set a new record, too. Then he won the Players Championship and the

“Anytime you can be compared to Tiger is really special, but the guy stands alone [atop] our game.” — SCOTTIE SCHEFFLER

Scottie Scheffler

59

Breaking 60 for 18 holes is supposed to be pretty hard and rare. **Hayden Springer** got a 59 in July in Illinois. He was not alone, however. Springer's career day was the eighth sub-60 18-hole score in tournaments around the world in the first half of 2024.

LIV Update

Another big PGA star moved to the competing LIV Golf tour. Former No. 1–ranked **Jon Rahm** of Spain signed with LIV Golf for the 2024 season. However, the biggest news in the cold war between LIV Golf and the PGA Tour was the lack of news. The two sides took a time-out from arguing in late 2023. They were supposed to agree to join forces, but it hadn't happened by the time we had to finish this book. Golf fans are still wondering what the future holds!

Masters—only the second golfer in history to complete that double in the same year. The first? You guessed it, Woods in 2001.

Pro Move

Golfers can make more than a million dollars for winning a PGA Tour event these days. In January 2024, **Nick Dunlap** won the American Express tournament in La Quinta, California, and got . . . a nice trophy. Dunlap didn't receive any money for his win because he was competing as an amateur. Only 20, Dunlap was the 2023 US Amateur champ. That got him a special invite to play the pros in the American Express event. He stunned the competition by recording a 60 in the third round to take the lead and won by one stroke. He was the first amateur to win on the PGA Tour since **Phil Mickelson** in 1991. He's now a pro and can accept future winnings!

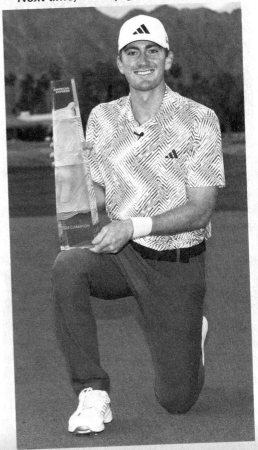

Next time, Dunlap gets a check, too!

Men's 2024 Majors

Scheffler was master of the Masters.

MEN'S 2024 MAJOR CHAMPIONS

MASTERS	**Scottie Scheffler**
PGA CHAMPIONSHIP	**Xander Schauffele**
US OPEN	**Bryson DeChambeau**
BRITISH OPEN	**Xander Schauffele**

Best Man

The Masters, played in Augusta, Georgia, challenges every part of a golfer's game. It was no surprise, then, that the man playing the best golf of 2024 was the best player at the Masters. World No. 1 **Scottie Scheffler** of the United States beat Sweden's **Ludvig Åberg** by four shots to win his second green jacket.

How Low Can You Go?

Xander Schauffele of the United States was the wire-to-wire winner of the PGA Championship. But it wasn't easy! Schauffele went in front with an opening-round 62. Two-time Major winner **Collin Morikawa** closed the gap and eventually pulled even through three rounds. Morikawa fell back on Sunday, but a new challenger emerged: **Bryson DeChambeau**, who shot a final-round 64 and pulled even on the last hole. But Schauffele birdied the 18th to win and set a Majors scoring record of 21 under par.

Nailed It!

Ahead by one shot on the 18th hole of the final round of the 2024 US Open, DeChambeau faced a long shot from a sand bunker. He needed to get the ball onto the green, then make the putt to win. DeChambeau hit "possibly my best golf shot of my entire life." He knocked the ball to within four feet of the hole, then drained the putt to win his second US Open.

British Open

Schauffele became only the sixth player ever to win the PGA and the British Open in the same year. He had to battle high winds and rain at the course in Scotland. In the final round, he shot a tournament-low 65 to win by two shots. He called that last 18 holes the "best round I've ever played."

Women's 2024 Majors

High Five!

Nelly Korda capped her record-tying five-match winning streak with a win at the Chevron Championship. She shot a steady 68-69-69-69 and finished two strokes ahead of Sweden's **Maja Stark** to win her second career Major.

Birdie Binge

Very low scores were tough to find at the 2024 US Women's Open. Only two players broke par over the four days of play. Even Korda, the hottest player in golf, ballooned to an opening-round 80. (She bounced back with a 70 in Round 2, but missed the cut.) That made **Yuka Saso**'s back nine on Sunday even more impressive.

Saso's fab final round earned the win.

WOMEN'S 2024 MAJOR CHAMPIONS	
CHEVRON CHAMPIONSHIP	**Nelly Korda**
WOMEN'S PGA CHAMPIONSHIP	**Amy Yang**
US WOMEN'S OPEN	**Yuka Saso**
EVIAN CHAMPIONSHIP	**Ayaka Furue**
WOMEN'S BRITISH OPEN	**Lydia Ko**

The Philippines-born golfer, who represents Japan, birdied four holes to beat **Hinako Shibuno**, also of Japan, by three shots.

Major Breakthrough

By mid-2024, South Korean **Amy Yang** had won 10 times in her pro career. The Majors were another story, though. She had several close calls, including two runner-up finishes at the US Women's Open but no wins. That changed at the 2024 Women's PGA Championship. Yang got a key birdie on the first hole of the final round to put her three shots clear of the field. She ended the day with her first Major title.

The Force Was with Her

A month before the 2024 Evian Championship in France, Japan's **Ayaka Furue** discovered *Star Wars*. She became such a fan that she began repeating to herself, "May the Force be with you." It was! Furue played the final five holes in five-under-par to win her first Major championship, capped with a 12-foot eagle putt on the final hole to win by one shot!

TENNIS

ON TOP OF THE WORLD
Coco Gauff's powerful forehand helped the young American rise to No. 2 in the world rankings in 2024.
(See page 173.)

2023 Tour Champs

WTA Finals

Poland's Iga Świątek entered the WTA Finals ranked No. 2, but after a dominating week at the Finals in Mexico, she was back to No. 1. Świątek breezed through her three matches in group play, then beat Aryna Sabalenka of Belarus, the reigning No. 1, in the semifinal. The final was even more lopsided. Świątek routed No. 5 Jessica Pegula of the United States, who had already beaten the world No. 1 (Sabalenka), No. 3 (Coco Gauff), and No. 4 (Elena Rybakina) players in the tournament. Świątek didn't lose a set the entire tournament—no one had done that since Serena Williams in 2012.

ATP Finals

Novak Djokovic of Serbia won the ATP Finals in Italy in November 2023 for the seventh time in his career. That broke a tie with legendary Roger Federer for the most ever. At 36, Djokovic also became the oldest winner of the event, surpassing the mark he set one year earlier. "Joker" hit a speed bump in group play when he dropped a three-set, 38-game thriller to Italian Jannik Sinner, but he still made it through to the final. It was a rematch with Sinner, and Djokovic won in straight sets. Djokovic wrapped up a year in which he went 55–6 and won three Grand Slam titles. "It's one of the best seasons I've had in my life, no doubt," he said.

Most Career Wins IN THE ATP FINALS

PLAYER	TITLES
Novak **DJOKOVIC**	7
Roger **FEDERER**	6
Ivan **LENDL**	5
Pete **SAMPRAS**	5

Djokovic capped off a great year in Italy.

Women's 2024 Grand Slams

TWICE AS NICE

Aryna Sabalenka of Belarus made back-to-back wins at the Australian Open; she got her first Grand Slam win there in 2023. Her booming serve and power game are well-suited to the hard courts of Melbourne. She won her first match 6–0, 6–1 in less than an hour! She won the final over Zheng Qinwen of China 6–3, 6–2. Sabalenka won all 14 sets she played in the tournament, dropping a total of only 31 games along the way.

2024 WOMEN'S GRAND SLAMS	
AUSTRALIAN OPEN	Aryna Sabalenka
FRENCH OPEN	Iga Świątek
WIMBLEDON	Barbora Krejcikova
US OPEN	Aryna Sabalenka

Krejcikova celebrates a winning point!

CLAY MASTER

With a win in the French Open after winning clay events in Madrid and Rome, Iga Świątek completed a rare triple. Only Serena Williams, in 2013, did it before. The Polish star had to survive a close call early in the French event. In the second round, she faced a match point against Naomi Osaka of Japan. Świątek fought off that point, then came back to win the match. Świątek won the final over Jasmine Paolini of Italy. It was Świątek's fourth French Open title and third in a row.

SOLO EFFORT

Barbora Krejcikova had a French Open title and a high world ranking in singles. But she was a bigger superstar in doubles, with 10 Grand Slam wins. At Wimbledon in 2024, she added another singles title. At the event near London, 11 of the top 12 seeds failed to reach the quarterfinals, so the tournament was thrown wide open. Krejcikova took advantage. She reached the final against No. 7–seed Jasmine Paolini, and won 6–4 in the third set.

Men's 2024 Grand Slams

VIVA ITALIA!

Through 2023, no Italian man had won a Grand Slam singles title since Adriano Panatta way back in 1976 at the French Open. After the first two sets of the 2024 Australian Open final, Italy's Jannik Sinner trailed Russia's Daniil Medvedev. Would the Italian streak continue? No! Sinner stormed back to win the final three sets and end his country's drought. The match was also the first time in 19 years that none of the Big Three—Novak Djokovic, Roger Federer, or Rafael Nadal—played in the final of the Australian Open. Sinner became the first Italian player ever to reach No. 1 in the world rankings.

Alcaraz goes full stretch for this shot on French Open red clay.

SPAIN REIGNS . . . IN FRANCE

For years, the French Open was Nadal's playground. The great Spanish star won a record 14 times at Roland-Garros near Paris—all since 2005. He was injured in 2023 and lost in his farewell match in 2024. So the next great Spanish star stepped up in his place. Carlos Alcaraz outlasted Germany's Alexander Zverev in five sets to win a Grand Slam title for his third consecutive season.

EYE ON THE PRIZE

At the 2024 Wimbledon tournament, Alcaraz reached the finals of a Grand Slam for the fourth time. And for the fourth time, he won. He also foiled Djokovic's chance at winning a third-straight Wimbledon title, which would have given the Serbian star a record-tying eighth career win. "It was all about Carlos," Djokovic said. "He was the dominant force on the court and deserved to win."

2024 MEN'S GRAND SLAMS

AUSTRALIAN OPEN	**Jannik Sinner**
FRENCH OPEN	**Carlos Alcaraz**
WIMBLEDON	**Carlos Alcaraz**
US OPEN	**Jannik Sinner**

At the Net: 2024

De Groot was on a winning binge!

Sir Andy

The Big Three—Novak Djokovic, Roger Federer, and Rafael Nadal—dominated men's tennis in the late 2010s and early 2020s. But before there was the Big Three, there was the Big Four: Andy Murray was included with those other superstars. Murray was just 17 when he turned pro in 2005. In 2013, he became a hero in Great Britain (he was born in Scotland) when he became the first British men's player in 77 years to win the Wimbledon singles title. He won again in 2016, and later

So long to Sir Andy after a great career!

Unstoppable

Who is the most dominant player—man or woman—in tennis? It's wheelchair tennis star Diede de Groot of the Netherlands. De Groot beat Aniek Van Koot, also of the Netherlands, at Wimbledon for her 15th Grand Slam singles title in a row! It gave her 23 for her career, too. De Groot also has 19 Grand Slam titles in doubles. In 2022, she won the full Grand Slam—all four singles titles in one year. Then she did it again in 2023! By the middle of 2024, her overall match-winning streak was at 145!

Paes exults after one of his many career wins.

Tennis Hall of Fame

Leander Paes, Vijay Armitraj, and Richard Evans joined the International Tennis Hall of Fame in Newport, Rhode Island, in 2024. Paes, from India, is one of the greatest doubles players ever. He won 18 Grand Slam titles in doubles and mixed doubles from 1999 to 2015. Armitraj first made a name for himself as a player in the 1970s but was elected to the Hall of Fame for his role as a broadcaster and administrator. The journalist Evans also was elected in the Contributor category. Paes and Armitraj are the first inductees from India, bringing the number of countries represented in the Hall of Fame to 28.

rose to No. 1 in the world rankings. In 2019, he was knighted by Prince Charles (now King Charles III), officially becoming Sir Andy Murray. Murray retired at the Olympics in 2024 after playing his final match there.

No. 2 . . . and Rising

United States star Coco Gauff is on a roll. She closed the 2023 Grand Slam season by winning the singles title at the US Open. Gauff, who was born in Atlanta, was only 19 when she became the first American woman to win the Open since Sloane Stephens in 2017, and the first American teenager since Serena Williams in 1999. Gauff kept rolling in 2024! In spring 2024, a couple of months after her 20th birthday, Gauff set a record for the most career WTA 1000 wins for anyone younger than 21. At the French Open in June, she teamed with Katerina Siniakova to win her first Grand Slam doubles title. And after reaching the singles semifinals, Gauff rose to No. 2 in the world!

Serena with Superpowers!

Williams is a real-life superhero. Millions have been inspired by her rise from the public tennis courts of Southern California to becoming her sport's GOAT. In 2024, an ESPN+ documentary came out that revealed Williams is a huge follower of DC Comics and its many (non-tennis-playing) superheroes, such as Batman, Superman, Wonder Woman, and more! Wonder Woman vs. Serena would be an awesome tennis match!

OTHER WORLD CHAMPIONS

CHAMPIONS AGAIN

Australian captain Pat Cummins was fantastic in the Cricket World Cup championship game. He surprised fans when he chose to let India bat first. His gamble paid off, as the Aussies were able to chase down India's runs when they got their turn. While bowling, Cummins also got India's star Virat Kohli out!

Cricket World Cup

In late November 2023, more than a billion sports fans turned their eyes to India for the Cricket World Cup. Compared to sports like baseball, football, and basketball, cricket is not a big deal in the United States. But in places like India, Australia, England, South Africa, and Pakistan, cricket is bigger than most other sports combined. The sport's World Cup is held every four years.

Cricket is a bat-and-ball game. Teams of 11 players compete on a huge field. Bowlers throw a rock-hard ball toward batters. The batters try to keep the ball from whacking into three small sticks behind them. If they hit the ball, they can run between two opposite sets of sticks to score a run. Longer hits can score 4 or 6 runs. The bowler can knock over the sticks (called wickets), kind of like a strikeout in baseball. Or, fielders can catch the ball to get batters out. There's a lot more to it than that, but those are the basics.

The World Cup in India was a version of the sport called One Day International (ODI). This form of the sport has each team throwing only up to 300 balls to the opponent. After both teams have batted, the team with the most runs wins.

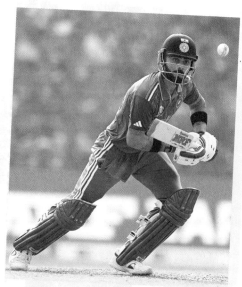

Kohli was terrific batting for India.

it past South Africa. The game was the closest played in the entire World Cup. Australia's bowlers held South Africa to a low total, and then its batters did just enough to win.

India 397, New Zealand 327

India's **Virat Kohli** led the way with 117 runs in a dominant win. It was the 50th time in his career that Kohli had topped 100 runs (called a "century" in cricket), setting a new ODI record.

Australia 215, South Africa 212

In the other semifinal, Australia just made

Australia 241, India 240

Fans in India got exactly what they wanted for the final—their hometown team, which had won 10 straight matches, against Australia, a five-time World Cup champ. But the loud and loyal fans didn't get their final wish. Australia won its sixth World Cup thanks to great batting from **Travis Head** and lights-out bowling by captain **Pat Cummins**. Kohli was named player of the tournament, though, setting a new World Cup record with 765 total runs.

Rugby World Cup

Rugby is another sport popular around the world that is not as big in the United States. In late 2023, the world's 20 best rugby national teams met in France for the World Cup. This event will be held in the United States in 2031, so we should start paying attention!

In the Rugby World Cup, teams have 15 players each. They move the ball up and down the field by running with it and kicking it. In rugby, points are scored with a "try," which is touching the ball down in one of the end zones (that's where we get "touchdown" from in American football). Teams can also score by kicking the ball through uprights. It's a hard-hitting, fast-moving sport.

At the World Cup, the 20 teams were split into four pools, with the top two in each making it through to the knockout stage. In pool play, France, Ireland, Wales, and England each finished without losing a match. Wales got a big 40-6 win over Australia in pool play, thanks to 23 points from **Gareth Anscombe**.

Rugby action includes exciting flying tackles like this by France against South Africa.

Pollard's kicks made South Africa champs.

Owen Farrell had four penalty kicks (worth three points each) for England's points. After a try by South Africa put them only two points behind, Handré Pollard hit a penalty kick for the winning score with just a few minutes left.

FINAL

South Africa 12, New Zealand 11

For the third straight game, South Africa won by just one point. But that one point was enough to give them their second World Cup championship in a row. It was also their fourth overall, a new record. New Zealand lost a player to a red card early, but the team kept the game tight even one man down. It was a very physical match with little scoring. Pollard had four penalty kicks for all of South Africa's points. New Zealand had a chance to win late, but their penalty kick fell short.

Australia is a two-time champ, but they didn't make the final eight after Portugal shocked Fiji for its first-ever win. That left Australia a few points shy of moving on.

SEMIFINALS

New Zealand 44, Argentina 6

Will Jordan scored three tries to lead the All Blacks to a big win. It was the second-largest point difference ever in a World Cup semifinal. New Zealand earned a spot in its record fifth World Cup final.

South Africa 16, England 15

England was ahead 15-6 only to watch South Africa storm back for the win.

Jordan dives in for a try against Argentina.

Winter X Games

Here are some of the highlights of this annual ski-and-snowboard extravaganza! It was held in Aspen, Colorado, in January 2024.

Marvelous Mia

Mia Brookes is only 17, but she was the gold medal winner in Snowboard Slopestyle. She had the three highest runs and also became the first woman to land a 1440. That's four complete spins in the air!

Record Ties

Two-time Olympic champ **Chloe Kim** added her seventh X Games gold in SuperPipe to a very crowded trophy cabinet. The win tied her for most X Games wins ever in this event. In the men's event, **Scotty James** won his third straight gold. That also ties an X Game all-time best!

Gold for Red

American snowboarder **Red Gerard** earned his first X Games gold medal with a terrific run in the Slopestyle event.

First-Time Event

Women got to take part in the Knuckle Huck event in 2024 for the first time. In this event, athletes zoom over large humps in the snow, showing off creative midair moves. Japan's **Kokomo Murase** took home the gold in the snowboard version (she got a second gold in Snowboard Big Air). **Olivia Asselin** of Canada won the ski Huck.

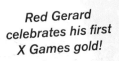

Red Gerard celebrates his first X Games gold!

Summer X Games

A little fog in Ventura, California, didn't keep action-sports fans from packing the venues at the Summer X Games. They watched skateboarders, BMX riders, and Moto X riders perform incredible feats. Here are some highlights.

She's Only Nine!

Skateboarder **Mia Kretzer** will have a pretty good souvenir to take to her elementary school class in Australia. She became the youngest X Games gold medalist ever when she won the women's Best Trick event.

Old Guy Rules!

Tom Schaar won the Skateboard Vert event, soaring to his third X Games gold medal. But it was his first since way back in 2014, when he was only 14! Another "old" guy, **Nyjah Huston**, 29, won the men's Skateboard Street Best Trick. His 14th X Games gold moves him into second place all-time.

All-Around Excellence

With gold in the BMX Street event, **Kevin Peraza** continued his dominance. He is the only rider ever with X Games gold in Street, Dirt, and Park!

Rising Skateboard Sun

Athletes from Japan ruled the women's skateboard Best Trick and Street events. The top four finishers in each were from that country. **Miyu Ito** won Street while **Yumeka Oda** took Best Trick.

Kretzer showed her stuff on the vert ramp.

Busy Day

On the third and final day of the event, skater **Arisa Trew** won a pair of golds. Like Mia, she is from Australia, but she's an "ancient" 14 years old! Arisa won the Vert and Park events, showing off her versatility and style!

Para Athletics

Note: This book had to print before the Paralympics were held after the Summer Olympics in Paris in September 2024. But we are happy to be able to share other athletic successes by differently abled athletes.

Para Athletics

A series of seven track-and-field meets in early 2024 matched the best wheelchair racers and other track-and-field athletes. Here are some of the highlights of the World Championship event held in Kobe, Japan.

→ China led the way with 33 gold medals. Sprinter **Wen Xiaoyan** broke two world records, while javelin thrower **Sun Pengxiang** broke a men's record in that event.

→ Several countries earned their first gold medals. **Noemi Alphonse** of Mauritius won a women's sprint event, while **Darlenys de la Cruz Severino** raced home with a gold for the Dominican Republic. Other first-time gold winners came from South Africa, Costa Rica, Iran, and Mexico.

→ Two British athletes set records. **Aled Davies** earned his 10th gold medal in the shot put, the most ever. Wheelchair racer **Hannah Cockroft** won two races to bring her record-setting career gold total to 16.

→ Brazil won four golds in one day! A highlight was the come-from-behind win by **Júlio Cesar Agripino dos Santos** in the men's 1500-meter, in a championship-record time.

→ US athletes won 24 medals, highlighted by a silver-bronze result in a 200-meter sprint for **Sydney Barta** and **Beatriz Hatz**.

Cockroft is one of the all-time greats on the track.

and Swimming

World Para Swimming

Seven Para Swimming World Series meets were held before the Paris Olympics. The swimmers and divers used the events to get ready for Paris. Here are some highlights from the event held in Indianapolis in April 2024.

➔ American swimmers loved the home cooking! They led the way with 10 gold medals. **Elizabeth Marks** and **Olivia Chambers** earned two golds apiece.

➔ **Owen McNear** of the United States added gold in the 100m backstroke for a championship in his first big international meet.

➔ Colombia had a great event, led by four gold medals from **Nelson Crispin Corzo**.

Crispin Corzo won races in three strokes plus a medley (races with a mix of strokes).

➔ Swimmers from Mexico carried home 15 medals, including seven golds. **Nely Miranda Herrera** won one of them in the women's 50m breaststroke (to go with previous Paralympic golds).

➔ **Sebastian Massabie** of Canada set a world record in a heat of the 50m butterfly, but was upset in the final by Crispin Corzo.

➔ American swimming superstar **Jessica Long** added three new medals to her amazing career record. Since 2004, she has piled up an incredible 53 gold medals in Paralympic Games, plus 33 World Championship golds.

Chambers on her way to gold in the 200m individual medley.

Horse Racing

A longshot is a horse that is not expected to do well in a race. In all three Triple Crown races in 2024, longshots came in winners! **Mystik Dan** was an 18-to-1 chance in the Kentucky Derby, but he inched out two other horses to win. It was so close that officials had to study photos for several minutes to find the winning horse's nose! It was the first Derby win for veteran jockey **Brian Hernandez Jr.**

In the second Triple Crown race, the Preakness Stakes, **Seize the Grey** was one of the longest shots in the event. But under **Jamie Torres**, the horse galloped to the front and stayed there until the finish line. Seize the Grey's not-so-secret weapon was trainer **D. Wayne Lukas**. At age 88, Lucas earned his seventh Preakness win, second-most of all time.

Finally at the Belmont Stakes, winner **Dornoch** might have gotten some tips from one of its owners. **Jayson Werth** helped the Philadelphia Phillies win a baseball World Series before he got into owning horses. Dornoch was a big longshot at 17 to 1, but jockey **Luis Saez** guided the horse to victory over both Mystik Dan and Seize the Grey.

That's Kentucky Derby winner Mystik Dan on the far right, racing for the finish line!

Hungry during a long ride? Have a snack, like race leader Tadej Pogačar (in yellow).

2024 Tour de France

Tadej Pogačar of Slovenia could have taken a nice, easy ride on the final day of the Tour de France. After all, he had a five-minute lead over second-place **Jonas Vingegaard**. But you don't win this famous cycling race three times by taking it slow. Instead, Pogačar whipped through the final sprint almost 21 miles faster than any other rider! Pogačar's win on the final-day time trial clinched his third Tour de France championship. (Trivia time: Because the Olympics were set for Paris later in July, the race ended in Nice, France. It was the first time the Tour did not conclude in Paris since 1905!)

But Pogačar was not the only big story of this massive 2,173-mile (3,498-km) race that took 21 separate rides to finish!

For Vingegaard, even showing up was impressive. Earlier in the spring, he had a bad crash in another race. His injuries put him in the hospital for 12 days—but he almost won his third Tour in a row!

Biniam Girmay of Eritrea became the first rider from Africa to win a stage. Not only that, he won three stages and was the Tour's top sprinter.

British rider **Mark Cavendish** won his 35th stage at a Tour de France, setting a new record for most in a career.

World Cycling Championships

In August 2023, for the first time, many of the best bicycle riders gathered in Glasgow, Scotland, for the UCI Cycling World Championships. While there are other competitions for each kind of riding, at this event, champs were declared for road, track, and BMX events all at the same time. Organizers called it the biggest cycling event ever held, including more than 200 events in cycling and paracycling. Here are some highlights.

Roberts flew high for another gold!

* Great Britain led the way with 100 total medals, including 47 golds. It was followed by France and the Netherlands. The US team of cyclists was fifth with 36 medals (15 gold).

* **Bethany Shriever** won one of those golds for Great Britain, flashing across the line to win the women's BMX Elite race.

* **Mathieu van der Poel** of the Netherlands won the men's Elite Road Race even after he had a big crash late in the event. He got back on his bike and, with blood showing on his knee and on his side, raced to the finish line!

* **Ricardo Ten Argiles** of Spain has only one leg and both of his arms end at about his elbows. That did not stop him from winning gold in the Para-Track Scratch Race event.

* **Hannah Roberts** of the United States must have a very strong neck. Why? She keeps getting medals to wear! She won her fifth World Championship in BMX Freestyle Park in Scotland.

* Downhill mountain bike racers plunge down a steep track, fly over jumps, and skid around tight turns. It's fast and dangerous, but **Valentina Höll** of Austria became a two-time world champ, winning by more than two seconds.

Slalom superstar Shiffrin added to her all-time record of World Cup race wins in 2024.

Winter Sports Roundup

WORLD CUP SKIING

American skier **Mikaela Shiffrin** was already the most successful skier of all time. In 2024, she added to her amazing record with her eighth World Cup slalom championship. Her nine overall race wins also moved her career record total to 97! Because Shiffrin missed six weeks with an injury, she finished third overall to champion **Lara Gut-Behrami** of Switzerland, who also won Super G and giant slalom titles.

The overall men's champion was Austria's **Marco Odermatt**. He dominated the sport, winning season titles in downhill, Super G, and giant slalom. His total points were almost double those of the second-place finisher.

SKATING CHAMPS!

At the 2024 World Figure Skating Championships, American skaters brought home two gold medals! **Ilia Malinin** (left) won the men's singles for the first time. He has good skating genes: Both his parents were champions in their native Uzbekistan. In ice dancing, Americans **Madison Chock** and **Evan Bates** defended their world championship. **Kaori Sakamoto** of Japan was the women's singles champ, while **Deanna Stellato-Dudek** and **Maxime Deschamps** won the pairs for Canada.

CHAMPIONS!

NFL

GAME	SEASON	RESULT
LVIII	2023	**Kansas City** 25, **San Francisco** 22
LVII	2022	**Kansas City** 38, **Philadelphia** 35
LVI	2021	**L.A. Rams** 23, **Cincinnati** 20
LV	2020	**Tampa Bay** 31, **Kansas City** 9
LIV	2019	**Kansas City** 31, **San Francisco** 20
LIII	2018	**New England** 13, **L.A. Rams** 3
LII	2017	**Philadelphia** 41, **New England** 33
LI	2016	**New England** 34, **Atlanta** 28
50	2015	**Denver** 24, **Carolina** 10
XLIX	2014	**New England** 28, **Seattle** 24
XLVIII	2013	**Seattle** 43, **Denver** 8

Michigan QB J.J. McCarthy

NFL MOST VALUABLE PLAYER

2023	**Lamar Jackson**, Baltimore
2022	**Patrick MAHOMES**, Kansas City
2021	**Aaron RODGERS**, Green Bay
2020	**Aaron RODGERS**, Green Bay
2019	**Lamar JACKSON**, Baltimore
2018	**Patrick MAHOMES**, Kansas City
2017	**Tom BRADY**, New England
2016	**Matt RYAN**, Atlanta
2015	**Cam NEWTON**, Carolina
2014	**Aaron RODGERS**, Green Bay

COLLEGE FOOTBALL

2023 **MICHIGAN**		2017 **ALABAMA**
2022 **GEORGIA**		2016 **CLEMSON**
2021 **GEORGIA**		2015 **ALABAMA**
2020 **ALABAMA**		2014 **OHIO STATE**
2019 **LSU**		2013 **FLORIDA ST.**
2018 **CLEMSON**		2012 **ALABAMA**

Here's a handy guide to recent winners and champions of most of the major sports. They've all been celebrated in past editions of the YEAR IN SPORTS. But here they are all together again!

MLB

2023 Texas **RANGERS** 4, Arizona **DIAMONDBACKS** 1
2022 Houston **ASTROS** 4, Philadelphia **PHILLIES** 2
2021 Atlanta **BRAVES** 4, Houston **ASTROS** 2
2020 Los Angeles **DODGERS** 4, Tampa Bay **RAYS** 2
2019 Washington **NATIONALS** 4, Houston **ASTROS** 3
2018 Boston **RED SOX** 4, Los Angeles **DODGERS** 1
2017 Houston **ASTROS** 4, Los Angeles **DODGERS** 3
2016 Chicago **CUBS** 4, Cleveland **INDIANS** 3
2015 Kansas City **ROYALS** 4, New York **METS** 1
2014 San Francisco **GIANTS** 4, Kansas City **ROYALS** 3
2013 Boston **RED SOX** 4, St. Louis **CARDINALS** 2

MLB MOST VALUABLE PLAYER

	AL	NL
2023	SHOHEI **OHTANI**	RONALD **ACUÑA**, JR.
2022	AARON **JUDGE**	PAUL **GOLDSCHMIDT**
2021	SHOHEI **OHTANI**	BRYCE **HARPER**
2020	JOSÉ **ABREU**	FREDDIE **FREEMAN**
2019	MIKE **TROUT**	CODY **BELLINGER**
2018	MOOKIE **BETTS**	CHRISTIAN **YELICH**
2017	JOSÉ **ALTUVE**	GIANCARLO **STANTON**
2016	MIKE **TROUT**	KRIS **BRYANT**
2015	JOSH **DONALDSON**	BRYCE **HARPER**
2014	MIKE **TROUT**	CLAYTON **KERSHAW**

COLLEGE BASKETBALL

YEAR	MEN'S	WOMEN'S
2024	Connecticut	S. Carolina
2023	Connecticut	LSU
2022	Kansas	S. Carolina
2021	Baylor	Stanford
2020	Not played	Not played
2019	Virginia	Baylor
2018	Villanova	Notre Dame
2017	N. Carolina	S. Carolina
2016	Villanova	Connecticut
2015	Duke	Connecticut
2014	Connecticut	Connecticut
2013	Louisville	Connecticut

NHL

2024 **Panthers** 4, Canucks 3

2023 **Golden Knights** 4, Panthers 1

2022 **Avalanche** 4, Lightning 2

2021 **Lightning** 4, Canadiens 1

2020 **Lightning** 4, Stars 2

2019 **Blues** 4, Bruins 3

2018 **Capitals** 4, Golden Knights 1

2017 **Penguins** 4, Predators 2

PWHL

2024 **Minnesota** 3, Boston 2

A'ja Wilson and the Aces: Two in a row!

NBA

2024 **Boston Celtics**

2023 **Denver Nuggets**

2022 **Golden State Warriors**

2021 **Milwaukee Bucks**

2020 **Los Angeles Lakers**

2019 **Toronto Raptors**

2018 **Golden State Warriors**

2017 **Golden State Warriors**

2016 **Cleveland Cavaliers**

2015 **Golden State Warriors**

2014 **San Antonio Spurs**

WNBA

2024 _____

2023 **Las Vegas Aces**

2022 **Las Vegas Aces**

2021 **Chicago Sky**

2020 **Seattle Storm**

2019 **Washington Mystics**

2018 **Seattle Storm**

2017 **Minnesota Lynx**

2016 **Los Angeles Sparks**

2015 **Minnesota Lynx**

2014 **Phoenix Mercury**

MLS

2023	Columbus Crew
2022	Los Angeles FC
2021	Portland Timbers
2020	Columbus Crew
2019	Seattle Sounders FC
2018	Atlanta United
2017	Toronto FC
2016	Seattle Sounders FC

NWSL

2023	NY/NJ Gotham FC
2022	Portland Thorns
2021	Washington Spirit
2020	Canceled
2019	North Carolina Courage
2018	North Carolina Courage
2017	Portland Thorns FC
2016	Western New York Flash

FIFA WORLD PLAYER OF THE YEAR*

Year	Men	Women
2023	Lionel **Messi**	Aitana **Bonmati**
2022	Lionel **Messi**	Alexia **Putellas**
2021	Robert **Lewandowski**	Alexia **Putellas**
2020	Robert **Lewandowski**	Lucy **Bronze**
2019	Lionel **Messi**	Megan **Rapinoe**[#]
2018	Luka **Modrić**	**Marta**
2017	Cristiano **Ronaldo**	Lieke **Martens**
2016	Cristiano **Ronaldo**	Carli **Lloyd**[#]
2015	Lionel **Messi**	Carli **Lloyd**[#]
2014	Cristiano **Ronaldo**	Nadine **Keßler**

* was known as the FIFA Ballon d'Or [Golden Ball] from 2010 to 2015.   # from the United States

PGA PLAYER OF THE YEAR

2023	Scottie **Scheffler**
2022	Scottie **Scheffler**
2021	Patrick **Cantlay**
2020	Dustin **Johnson**
2019	Rory **McIlroy**
2018	Brooks **Koepka**
2017	Justin **Thomas**
2016	Dustin **Johnson**
2015	Jordan **Spieth**
2014	Rory **McIlroy**
2013	Tiger **Woods**

LPGA PLAYER OF THE YEAR

2023	Lilia **Vu**
2022	Lydia **Ko**
2021	Jin Young **Ko**
2020	Sei Young **Kim**
2019	Jin Young **Ko**
2018	Ariya **Jutanugarn**
2017	Sung Hyun **Park** and So Yeon **Ryu**
2016	Ariya **Jutanugarn**
2015	Lydia **Ko**
2014	Stacy **Lewis**
2013	Inbee **Park**

ATP PLAYER OF THE YEAR

2023	Novak **DJOKOVIC**
2022	Carlos **ALCARAZ**
2021	Novak **DJOKOVIC**
2020	Novak **DJOKOVIC**
2019	Rafael **NADAL**
2018	Novak **DJOKOVIC**
2017	Rafael **NADAL**
2016	Andy **MURRAY**
2015	Novak **DJOKOVIC**
2014	Novak **DJOKOVIC**
2013	Rafael **NADAL**

WTA PLAYER OF THE YEAR

2023	Iga **ŚWIĄTEK**
2022	Iga **ŚWIĄTEK**
2021	Ashleigh **BARTY**
2020	Sofia **KENIN**
2019	Ashleigh **BARTY**
2018	Simona **HALEP**
2017	Garbiñe **MUGURUZA**
2016	Angelique **KERBER**
2015	Serena **WILLIAMS**
2014	Serena **WILLIAMS**
2013	Serena **WILLIAMS**

NASCAR

2023	RYAN **BLANEY**
2022	JOEY **LOGANO**
2021	KYLE **LARSON**
2020	CHASE **ELLIOT**
2019	KYLE **BUSCH**
2018	JOEY **LOGANO**
2017	MARTIN **TRUEX JR.**
2016	JIMMIE **JOHNSON**
2015	KYLE **BUSCH**
2014	KEVIN **HARVICK**
2013	JIMMIE **JOHNSON**

INDYCAR

2023	ALEX **PALOU**
2022	WILL **POWER**
2021	ÁLEX **PALOU**
2020	SCOTT **DIXON**
2019	JOSEF **NEWGARDEN**
2018	SCOTT **DIXON**
2017	JOSEF **NEWGARDEN**
2016	SIMON **PAGENAUD**
2015	SCOTT **DIXON**
2014	WILL **POWER**
2013	SCOTT **DIXON**

FORMULA 1

2023	MAX **VERSTAPPEN**
2022	MAX **VERSTAPPEN**
2021	MAX **VERSTAPPEN**
2020	LEWIS **HAMILTON**
2019	LEWIS **HAMILTON**
2018	LEWIS **HAMILTON**
2017	LEWIS **HAMILTON**
2016	NICO **ROSBERG**
2015	LEWIS **HAMILTON**

DAYTONA 500 CHAMPIONS

2024	Will **BYRON**
2023	Ricky **STENHOUSE JR.**
2022	Austin **CINDRIC**
2021	Michael **MCDOWELL**
2020	Denny **HAMLIN**
2019	Denny **HAMLIN**
2018	Austin **DILLON**
2017	Kurt **BUSCH**
2016	Denny **HAMLIN**
2015	Joey **LOGANO**

INDY 500 CHAMPIONS

2024	Josef **NEWGARDEN**
2023	Josef **NEWGARDEN**
2022	Marcus **ERICSSON**
2021	Hélio **CASTRONEVES**
2020	Takuma **SATO**
2019	Simon **PAGENAUD**
2018	Will **POWER**
2017	Takuma **SATO**
2016	Alexander **ROSSI**
2015	Juan Pablo **MONTOYA**

Newgarden and his Indy winner's ring

Produced by Shoreline Publishing Group LLC
Santa Barbara, California
www.shorelinepublishing.com
President/Editorial Director: James Buckley, Jr.
Designed by Tom Carling, www.carlingdesign.com

The text for *Scholastic Year in Sports 2025* was written by
James Buckley, Jr.
Other writers: **Jim Gigliotti** (Golf and Tennis); **Beth Adelman** and **Craig Zeichner** (NHL); **Jacob Norling** (College Basketball).
Fact-checking: **Matt Marini** and **Ken Samelson**. Thanks, guys!
Thanks to team captain **Tiffany Colón**, the photo squad of **Emily Teresa** and **Marybeth Kavanagh**, and the superstars at Scholastic for all their championship work!
Photo research was done by the author.

● ●

Photography Credits